"What in the world is that?" He threw off his blanket and went to the north window, parted the faded, dusty curtains, and looked outside. "The saddle shed door blew open." He scowled and rubbed his chin with a finger. "I know I closed it. I think I closed it. Huh."

You know the one thing he didn't think about? You'll find out soon enough. I didn't think about it either.

The Case of the Prowling Bear

John R. Erickson

Illustrations by Gerald L. Holmes

Maverick Books, Inc.

MAVERICK BOOKS, INC.
Published by Maverick Books, Inc.
P.O. Box 549, Perryton, TX 79070
Phone: 806.435.7611
www.hankthecowdog.com

First published in the United States of America by Maverick Books, Inc. 2013.

1 3 5 7 9 10 8 6 4 2

Copyright © John R. Erickson, 2013

LIBRARY OF CONGRESS CONTROL NUMBER: 2013934606

978-1-59188-161-2 (paperback); 978-1-59188-261-9 (hardcover)

Hank the Cowdog® is a registered trademark of John R. Erickson.

Printed in the United States of America

For Baxter and Cindy Lou

CONTENTS

CHAPTER ONE

The Secret Donkey Report

It's me again, Hank the Cowdog. Let's get right to this business of the bear. I can tell you exactly when and how the rumors got started.

It was the first week in January, as I recall. Yes, it was the second week in January—long nights, cold gloomy days. Or was it February? On this ranch, there isn't much difference between January and February, so it doesn't matter.

The mystery began when it began, in the cold of winter, only on that particular day, it wasn't cold. In fact, it was warm and spring-like, almost sixty degrees. Slim shed his coat around nine o'clock that morning and shucked off his wool vest about an hour later.

Slim, Drover, and I were out feeding cattle. In

the dead of winter, it's something we do every day. We drive to the same pastures and pour out feed to the same cattle, who always give the impression that they've never eaten a bite of store-bought feed in their whole lives, which makes us wonder why we bother.

Let's face it. Cows are greedy, dumb, and have no sense of gertrude. Gratitude. They have no gertrude of gratitude. It doesn't matter how hard you work or how much feed you pour out for them, they're never happy and they always want more. Hence, don't stake your career on pleasing a cow. It won't happen.

We poured out feed in the first two pastures and were chugging along the county road, on our way to the next pasture. Drover stared off into the vapors of space. Slim hummed a tune and concentrated on his driving.

If this had been the middle of summer, he would have been swerving from one side of the road to the other, trying to smash those jumbo grasshoppers that get almost as big as a lizard. But this was wintertime (no grasshoppers for entertainment), so he had nothing to do but drive.

Me? I was in my usual position on the Shotgun Side of the pickup, and perhaps I had dozed off. Yes, I'm sure I had, because...well, active minds tend to doze when there isn't much to keep them occupied. But that changed all at once, when I heard the screech of brakes and went flying into the dashboard. Next thing I knew, I was sprawled on the floor with something lying on top of me.

It took me a moment to respond. "Battle stations! Code Three! We've been rammed! Flood tubes one and three! There's a dead body on my face!"

I pushed, shoved, and scrambled, and finally pried myself out from under the pile of corpses that had...huh? Okay, relax, false alarm. Ha ha. The pile of corpses turned out to be Drover, and he was still alive. Ha ha. Boy, sometimes the mind plays tricks.

I blinked my eyes and tried to put on a professional face. "What's the meaning of this, and why were you smashing my face?"

"Well, he slammed on the brakes and we ended up on the floor."

"Who slammed on the brakes?" I studied the face in front of me. When we had begun this conversation, I had seen two faces, but now they had merged into one. "Okay, you're Drover and Slim's the driver, but why did he slam the brakes and sling us to the floor?"

Drover shrugged and we both turned our gazes toward Slim Chance, the hired hand on this outfit. He was sitting behind the wheel, and looking a little...well, dazed, I guess you would say. After a moment, he said, "Dogs, you ain't going to believe this. Would you like to guess what just ran across the road?"

Oh brother. A rabbit? A coyote? Coon, fox, badger, reindeer, moose...what did we care?

He shook his head and let out a breath of air. "I think I'm wide awake and not any crazier than I was yesterday, but unless my eyes were playing tricks, I saw a *bear* run across the road."

He saw a BEAR run across the road? We didn't have bears in the Texas Panhandle. Bears lived in the mountains. We didn't have mountains. No mountains, no bears. I had no idea what he'd seen, but it hadn't been a bear.

"You don't believe me, do you?"

Of course we didn't believe him! I mean, the guy was famous for telling windy tales and pulling pranks on his dogs, right?

"Hank, I saw a bear, honest."

Okay, you saw a bear. I saw an elephant. Could we get on with the business of feeding cattle?

He put the pickup in gear and we drove on to

the next pasture. Drover had been silent up to this point, and now he said, "Berries don't grow in the wintertime."

"That's true. Your strawberries and your blackberries make fruit in the summer. If you live on berries, that's important information, but we don't eat them, so what's your point?"

"Well, he saw he said a berry in the road."

"Wait. *He saw he said?* That doesn't make sense. Perhaps you meant to say, 'He said he saw.'"

"That's what I said. I said, 'He said he saw.'"

"No, you said, 'He saw he said.'"

"Yeah, but he couldn't saw what he said until he said what he saw, and you can't saw words anyway."

I took a deep breath and searched for patience. "Drover, we seem to be having a little trouble communicating this morning. Let's go back to the beginning and try again."

"Yeah, but I forgot what we were talking about."

"Berries. You were talking about strawberries."

He gave me a loony stare. "Why would I talk about strawberries?"

"I have no idea. Wait, I remember. You said he said he saw a strawberry growing in the road."

A little flicker of light came on in his eyes. "Oh yeah. He said he saw a berry run across the road."

The air hissed out of my lungs. "Okay, let me address this in two parts. First, berries don't grow in the winter. Second, berries don't run across roads. And third, he didn't say 'berry,' he said '*bear*.'"

"Hee hee hee. It must be a joke. We don't have bears."

"Of course we don't have bears, but that's what he said, and I don't think he was kidding."

This threw us into a moment of troubled thought. Then Drover brightened. "Wait, here's an idea. Maybe he said 'burro' instead of 'bear.' They sound kind of the same: burro and bear."

"Hmmm. Actually, that makes a certain amount of sense. Yes, of course. He saw a donkey crossing the road."

"Yeah, and maybe his name was Donkey Hoety and somebody was trying to pin a tail on him."

"It all fits together, doesn't it? By George, I think we've finally figured it out. Slim saw a donkey crossing the road."

"Yeah, but I wonder why he crossed the road."

"That's easy. We just apply Higher Logic. Why does a chicken cross the road?"

He wadded up his face in a pose of deep concentration. "Well, let me think. To get to the other side?"

"Exactly, very good. Now let's move to the next step. If a chicken crosses the road to get to the other side, why does a donkey cross the road?"

He struggled with this one. "Well, let's see. 'Cause he's chasing the chicken?"

"No, absolutely wrong. Donkeys don't chase chickens."

"I wish you wouldn't ask me such hard questions."

"Drover, it's so obvious you can't see it, but I'll give you a hint. Chicken, road, donkey, road."

A big smile bloomed on his mouth. "Oh, I get it now. The chicken rode the donkey. Hee hee, boy, that was easy."

What can you say? Nothing. There are some events in our lives that can't be explained, and some dogs that can't be helped. "Nice work, son, you really nailed it."

"Thanks, but I couldn't have done it without your help."

"Right. It was a good hint, wasn't it? I'm glad you enjoyed it."

"Yeah, I love getting the right answers. It makes me tingle all over."

While he tingled all over, I stared out the window and wondered how this nincompoop had ended up on my staff. Just bad luck, I guess.

Where were we?

Oh yes, burros. We had unauthorized donkeys on the ranch, so I opened a new file, The Case of the Wandering Donkey, and our Special Crimes Division put out an APB for a four-legged, long-eared animal named "Donkey Hoety."

Oh, by the way, APB is our shorthand for All Points Bulletin. Is that impressive or what? You bet. You know, if the people on this outfit paid more attention to their dogs, things would run a lot smoother. But let's don't get started on that.

The point is that for the rest of the day, while Slim drove from pasture to pasture, Drover and I kept the whole ranch under surveillance. I mean, we left no stern untoned. We checked out every animal on the ranch, and compared them to our profiles of donkeys and burros.

You're probably wondering, "What's the difference between a donkey and a burro?" Great question. The answer is, they both have big ears. But the impoitant poink is that our surveillance of animals on the ranch turned up no unidentified donkeys or burros. At the end of our daily feed run, Donkey Hoety was still unaccounted for.

To be honest, it caused me to wonder if Slim actually had seen a donkey or if he'd been daydreaming. On this outfit, we're never sure.

CHAPTER TWO

An Evening of Fun and Entertainment

Well, there you have a rare glimpse of what goes on behind closed doors at the Security Division. A lot of people think that ranch dogs just sit around all day, scratching fleas and barking at birds. Ha. Far from it.

The truth is, we collect a vast amount of information every day. Some of it is reliable, some is just garbage. We have to sort through every bit of it, give it shape, and provide the kind of heavy duty analysis that brings it into hocus pocus.

Wait. Into *focus*, sharp focus. We rarely get involved in hocus pocus.

Come to think of it, what is hocus pocus? I'm not sure, so let's skip it.

Data analysis is one of the most difficult parts of this job, because we're surrounded by people who are dedicated to pulling pranks and goofing off. We dogs never know what to believe and are often left bewildered, faced with the challenge of trying to figure out if it's raining or Tuesday. Sometimes it's both, sometimes it's neither, and it's our job to sort it all out.

But the point is that the Security Division sifted through a mountain of data and started a file for The Case of the Wandering Donkey. In the space of a few short minutes, we had come up with a name for the suspect (Donkey Hoety) and a motive (he was looking for his tail).

It's pretty amazing what two dogs can do when they put their minds together, isn't it? You bet.

Late that afternoon, we made our way back to Slim's shack. Drover and I had recently moved the Security Division's command post from its normal location at ranch headquarters, down to Slim Chance's bachelor shack on the banks of Wolf Creek. We do this every year when the weather turns cold. We've found that our communications gear functions better at Slim's place, and you know how important it is to have all that high-tech equipment working in top shape.

Also, Slim let's his dogs stay in the house on cold winter nights, heh heh, and, well, that's a huge factor in keeping up the morale of the unit. Studies have shown that dogs who sleep inside houses with warm stoves perform 83% better than those who sleep on frozen gunny sack beds beneath gas tanks.

I mean, this isn't just the opinion of one dog who's got some skin in the game. This stuff has been studied and documented. If you want your Security Division to be sharp and alert, bring 'em inside and let 'em stretch out beside the friendly glow of a wood-burning stove.

Slim had his faults, but on the matter of Dogs In The House, he was on the cutting edge of ranch management. The man had learned that a happy, well-rested Security Division is the best investment a ranch can make.

Anyway, we made it back to Slim's place around sundown. In February, darkness comes early, around six o'clock, and it can be very dark. Maybe that seems obvious, that darkness is dark, but it's also true. Around here, our darkness is dark.

The fire in Slim's wood stove had died down to embers, so he brought in a load of chinaberry and mesquite wood, and chunked up the stove. Before long, the house was warm and cozy, and Slim set about making himself some supper.

He's a bachelor, you know, and doesn't spend a lot of time in the kitchen. His suppers usually come straight out of a can: hash, Vienna sausage, sardines, or mackerel, the stinkingest fish you can buy. It smells almost as bad as cat food. Don't eat his mackerel sandwiches.

But on this particular evening, he must have been feeling inspired, because he actually *cooked* something. Yes sir, he made a big pot of boiled chicken gizzards, added two bullion cubes to give them some flavor, and even dumped some rice into the pot.

Why chicken gizzards? Very few people will eat gizzards, so they're cheap, and that makes them perfect food for bachelor cowboys. Most folks grocery-shop for nutrition and taste. Bachelors shop for cheap.

Hey, and get this. After supper, he even spent some time cleaning up the kitchen. He swept all the crumbs off the dinner table and onto the floor, which is a smart thing to do. It keeps the mice from crawling around on your eating surface. Then he placed his dirty dishes into the freezer compartment of the refrigerator.

Smart move. Several rounds of food poisoning had taught him a valuable lesson about sanitation: if you don't freeze those dirty dishes, they'll come back to bite you.

Then we all moved into the living room and began an evening of fun and excitement. That's a joke. Long winter evenings at Slim's place weren't exactly electric experiences. We didn't do much. Drover stretched out on the floor, while I found a more comfortable spot on...

"Get out of my chair."

...on the floor beside Drover. Gee, what a grouch. Slim took the only comfortable chair in the house and settled into reading the latest issue of *Western Horseman* magazine. That lasted for about thirty minutes, then he got restless, went back into the kitchen, and made a batch of popcorn.

Somehow he managed to scorch the first batch, and we're talking about a cloud of smoke that filled the entire house. He had to open all the doors and windows to let the place air out, and by the time the smoke had cleared, the temperature in the house was about right for hanging a side of beef. Cold.

But he made another batch and ended up with a bowl of fluffy popcorn. He returned to his chair and crunched away on his evening treat, while Drover and I...well, we had some interest in this, you might say, and we took up positions at Slim's feet. There, we watched him eat. We moved our front paws up and down, licked our chops, thumped our tails on the floor (I did; Drover's tail was too short), and uttered Groans of Desire.

I don't often resort to Groans of Desire because, well, they sound a lot like begging, and I'm no beggar. But sometimes our people don't take hints and we have to dig into our bag of tricks.

We set up shop at his feet and launched ourselves into Groans of Desire. At first, they had no effect. He kept stuffing his face. Oh, he knew we wanted to share his popcorn, but he just grinned and kept eating.

We cranked up the Groans and at last he said, "Would y'all like to have some popcorn?"

You see what we have to put up with? OF COURSE WE WANTED SOME POPCORN! Any rock, tree, or fence post on the ranch would have known that we wanted some popcorn.

He grinned. "Okay, I'll make a deal. If you can catch it out of the air, I'll let you have some."

I turned to Drover. "What do you think, can we handle this?"

"Oh yeah, let's do it."

And that's what we did. For the next hour, we played Slow Pitch Popcorn. Slim did the pitching and we dogs did the catching, and you know what? We were pretty good at it. We muffed a few shots at the beginning (sometimes that popcorn will bounce off your nose, don't you see), but we got better with practice. By the end of the game, Slim was giving us long fly balls that went looping all the way up to the ceiling, and we snagged every one of them. Most of them.

Wow. It's pretty amazing what dogs can do, but around nine-thirty, we ran out of popcorn, and that ended our evening of fun and entertainment. Slim got up out of his chair and took a big stretch.

"Come on, dogs, it's time for y'all to answer the Call of the Wild." We followed him out on the porch. He pointed up at the moon. "Moon's got a ring around it, a sign the weather's fixing to change. Which reminds me. My pot's got a water ring and I need to soak it with Babbo."

Water ring? Babbo? It made no sense to me. One minute he was talking about the moon and the weather, and the next minute…I don't know, he'd switched to water and cooking pots and Babbo, whatever that might have been. You know, we dogs are doing well if we understand *half* of what our people say, and guess who always gets blamed for the communication failures. The dogs.

The truth is, our people mutter and mumble, talk to themselves, and never bother to explain anything. And with Slim, the lines of communication are even more snarled, because he spends half his time pulling pranks. He would rather play pathetic tricks on his dogs than...I don't know, eat popcorn, I suppose.

Do you remember the time he unbuttoned his shirt, pulled it up over his head, and buttoned it again? I remember it very well. It made him look like *a man without a head*, and you can imagine what he did with that. Naturally, I started growling, I mean, that's what a dog is supposed to do when he sees a headless man on his ranch, right? I growled and barked, so he made claws with his hands and came after me, and...

We don't need to go into all the details. The point is that we dogs never know what to believe or what's coming next, so it wasn't my fault that I didn't pay any attention to his statement about pots, rings, and Babbo. As you will see, it almost cost me my life, but that's getting the cart in front of the wagon.

Drover and I answered The Call of the Wild, and Slim let us back into the house.

He said good night, and went off to his bedroom. We curled up in front of the stove, and the next thing we knew...

You probably thought I was going to say, "The next thing I knew, it was daylight." Not quite. The next thing I knew, it was about four o'clock in the morning. The stove had burned down to embers, and the house had gotten cold.

This problem can be corrected if a certain member of the household will get out of his warm bed, collect an arm-load of wood from the wood pile on the porch, and chunk up the stove. Dogs don't do wood, and sometimes Slim doesn't either. He lets the fire die down and covers up his head with a wool blanket, and the house gets cold.

In other words, this was not a Dog Problem. It was a Human Problem, but we dogs were left to cope with the aftermaths of the consequences. We shivered on a cold floor, and tried to sleep.

Drover was making his usual orchestra of weird sounds: chirps, hicks, snorts, grunts, and whistles. Who can sleep through such noise? Well, I tried. That's where we were—me trying to sleep and Drover making more noise than a room full of monkeys.

But then he did something unusual. He sat up and said, "Hank, I'm thirsty."

I had put my calls on hold, but somehow this one got through, and I replied, "Rubbish. If you were thirty, the sandwiches would be growing sideways."

The voice came again. "No, I said I'm *thirsty*."

"That's impossible. We haven't had Wednesday yet and Thursday doesn't grow on trees."

"Hank, wake up. You're babbling."

I lifted my head and saw...something, maybe a dog. Yes, it was a dog. "If Babylon is such a great place, why don't you move there and leave me alone?" I blinked my eyes. "Where are we?"

"We're in Slim's living room. I'm Drover, remember me?"

I narrowed my eyes and studied him. "We've met before?"

"About ten thousand times."

"No wonder I'm so tired." I struggled to my feet and took a few steps. "Something's wrong with my legs. I'm walking crooked."

"You're still asleep."

"I am not asleep. I've been awake for hours." I stopped and turned to face him.

"Don't we play on the same popcorn team?"

"Yep, that's me. Are you awake now?"

"Of course I'm awake. What is the point of this conversation?"

"I'm thirsty."

At last the pieces of the puzzle were beginning to fall into place. In the middle of the night, I was talking to Drover, and he was thirsty.

CHAPTER THREE

The Poisoned
Toilet Bowl

Ilooked into his eyes and felt that I was peering
into two cardboard tubes with nothing on the
other end. That might sound cruel, but it was
true.

"You woke me up to tell me that you're thirsty?
That's ridiculous. How can you be thirsty in the
middle of the night?"

"I don't know, but I am."

"Why didn't you get a drink before you went to
bed?"

"I was afraid I'd wet the floor."

"Oh brother. Drover, you are the most...Slim
keeps a water bowl beside the back door. Instead
of waking me up, why didn't you just go to the
water bowl and get yourself a drink?"

22

"Well, I tried but it was empty. I guess he forgot to fill it."

"Then why didn't you do the obvious—walk into the bathroom and drink out of the pot? That's what pots are for."

He rolled his eyes around. "Well...it's dark in there and I'm scared of the dark."

"Oh brother. So you expect me to give you an escort into the bathroom? Is that what you're saying?" He nodded. "You can forget that, pal. I'm off duty and I don't give escorts in the middle of the..." I heaved a sigh. "But if you don't get your drink, you'll be whining all night and I'll never get back to sleep."

"I'm sorry to be such a burden."

"If you're so sorry, quit being a burden. Drink water during the daylight hours, like every other dog in America. Come on, let's get this over with."

"I sure appreciate this."

"Please hush." I headed down the dark hallway and stopped at the bathroom door. Drover followed. "Okay, this is the bathroom. The pot is over there. Get your drink and hurry up."

He crept into the bathroom. A moment later, I heard his voice. "Uh oh."

"What does that mean?"

"Somebody put the lid down on the pot."

"Impossible. Bachelors never do that."

"Well, somebody did. Come look."

There was just enough moonlight coming through the window so that I could see the device. And, much to my surprise, Drover had gotten it right. Somebody had put down the lid.

Drover was fretting. "What'll we do now?"

"We? You're the one who wants the drink. Figure it out."

"Yeah, but…"

"Drover, put your nose under the lid, lift it up, and stick your head inside."

"What if my head gets caught?"

"It won't get caught. The lid is on hinges."

"Well, I guess I could try."

"Give it a try." I licked my lips and realized that they were dry. "As a matter of fact, I'm kind of thirsty myself, so make it snappy."

Drover slipped his nose under the lid, poked his head inside the bowl, and began lapping. The sound of water produced mental pictures of a pool of crystal clear spring water on a hot afternoon. I was ready for a drink.

"Are you done yet?" He removed his head and I noticed that he was making a sour face. "What's wrong?"

"I don't know. The water has a funny taste. I

don't want any more."

"Good. It's my turn."

"I thought you weren't thirsty."

"I wasn't until I had to stand here, listening to you guzzle."

"You know, Hank, I'm not sure you ought to drink that water. It has a soapy taste."

"Get out of the way."

I pushed him aside, slipped my nose under the lid, lifted it up several inches, and plunged my entire head, face, and nose into the porcelain bowl. Then, with the wooden seat resting against the top of my head, I began lapping cool spring water.

Okay, maybe it had an odd taste, but ranch dogs don't worry about such little details. Hey, we're the same guys who drink out of stock tanks, creeks, and mud puddles.

Wow, great water, and it really hit the spot. I drank my fill and at that point, all I had to do was...HUH?

Holy smokes, I couldn't get my head out! See, the toilet seat was resting on the top of my head, and when I tried to back out, the stupid lid became wedged behind my ears.

Actually, there was never any chance of me drowning, but let me tell you something. If your head has never been trapped inside a toilet bowl, don't laugh at someone who's been through such an ordeal.

It was scary. My mind was telling me it wasn't a big deal, but there I was in this dark place, hearing my own voice in an echo chamber. It sounded like...I don't know, like a voice from the Bottomless Pit of Doom.

"Drover, do something! We have a Code Three. I can't get my head out of here!"

"I tried to tell you."

"Hurry up and do something!"

"Help, murder!"

What's a dog to do? I went into Full Reverse on all engines, and we're talking about all four legs digging deep and throwing up sparks in the night. After a terrible struggle, my head popped free and...well, I went roaring backwards, hit the wall, and ended up on the floor. Two towels fell off the towel rack and landed on top of my head.

Whew! I had survived the experience, but then...oops. The bathroom light came on and I found myself looking into the eyes of...gulp... Slim Chance. There he stood in his red one-piece long john underwear—hair down in his face and wearing an expression that suggested...irritation.

Mad. He looked mad and burned me up with

a hostile glare. "Hank, were you drinking out of the pot?"

Why had he addressed that question to *me*? What about the little ninny who had started the whole thing? It was then I realized that Drover had vanished, leaving me all alone to face Slim's wrath.

I held my head at a proud angle and gave him a direct gaze that said, "Of course we were drinking out of the pot. What did you expect? You fed us dry popcorn and didn't put out any water for us, and we chose not to perish from thirst. I got my head caught in the commode, but managed to survive. Thanks for all your concern, and you can go back to bed."

Slim rolled his eyes and shook his head. "Birdbrain. I closed the lid on the pot for a reason."

A reason?

"I put Babbo in the water."

Babbo?

"Cleanser. You drank *toilet bowl cleanser*."

Huh?

Hmmm. Perhaps that explained the odd taste. Well, how was I supposed to know? Slim wasn't famous for cleaning anything in his house, and who would have guessed...

Uh oh. Something was happening in the depths of my stomach. It came suddenly, in a rush and a blur. My head began moving up and down, and I heard odd noises coming from deep inside my body.

"Ump. Ump. Ump."

Slim's soggy eyes burst into flames. "Get out of here! Outside, quick!" He made a dash for the front door and I heard him yell, "This way, pooch, outside!"

You know, in moments of crisis, we sometimes make peculiar decisions. Later, we look back on our actions and wonder why we did them. See, I knew he wanted me to make a dash for the front door and to finish off the drama in his yard. It would have been the sensible thing to do, and yet...

And yet in that tense, stressful moment when I had to choose between going left toward the front door, or going right toward the darkness and solitude of Slim's bedroom, I, uh, made a hard right turn and went galloping down the hall to the bedroom.

Looking back, I can only guess that I couldn't bear the thought of purging my system in front of an audience. (There's that word again: *bear*. Was that a clue? Maybe not). Yes, it was my sense of modesty that drove me into the bedroom. I was ashamed that I had guzzled tainted water; ashamed that I had ignored the little warnings of my taste buds; ashamed that the nasty stuff had made me ill.

And most of all, I was ashamed...no, I was *furious* that Drover had sat there like a stump and allowed me to drink poison!

Okay, maybe he'd muttered something about a "funny taste," but he should have warned me that the stuff was contanimated...laminated... concreeminated...he should have warned me that someone had tampered with our water supply.

But he didn't, and there I stood in Slim's bedroom. My mind was fogged and my gizzardly depths cried out for some kind of release. I had to do something, so I did what brave American dogs have been doing for centuries.

I crawled under the bed.

There, I found the privacy I needed for this ordeal, a place where I could correct my mistakes in a quiet spot and spare myself the humilification of being mocked by a crowd of small minds. If I was lucky, nobody would ever find the uh...mess.

And, you know, it worked out pretty well. The first ten seconds were violent and messy, but then it was over. I had faced the crisis head-on, and now it was just an unpleasant memory.

Good news, but things got even better when I was able to express this Learning Situation in a wonderful song. Would you like to hear it?

Be Careful When You Drink From the Pot

Be careful when you drink from the pot.
You might think the water's pure when it's not.
A thirsty dog is full of hope
But if the bowl is full of soap,
It changes the equation quite a lot.

It's confusing when a bachelor displays
A sudden interest in Good Housekeeping
ways.
Slim rarely cleans his house,
Fussy mice have all moved out,
So what's the deal…Babbo in the commode?

Just when you think you know your people to
the core,
They change their patterns and you find there
is more:
Hidden things with no suggestion
That can wreck a dog's digestion.
Makes you wonder if they do this for a joke.

How's a dog supposed to know what to
    think?
Is the water in the house fit to drink?
Tainted water starts a blizzard
When it ends up in your gizzard.
It can rattle your insides like an earth...
    quake.

The moral of this song is "Dogs Beware!"
Choose your source of drinking water with
    great care.
If the lid's down on the pot,
It's a sign that you should not
Stick your head inside and guzzle like a hog.

If the lid's down on the pot,
It's a sign that you should not
Stick your head inside and guzzle like a hog.

CHAPTER FOUR

Bears Inside
the House!

I told you it was a wonderful song. Sweet, tender, great message, filled with meaning. Awesome.

I emerged from my sanctuary, ready to begin my life all over again. I felt much better, took a big stretch, gave myself a shake, and trotted toward the living room. I had a feeling that Slim would be looking for me. Sure enough, he was, and wearing a deep scowl.

"What were you doing back there?"

Me? Oh, nothing. I just made a wrong turn, is all.

"You need to go outside."

Fine. No problem.

I went out the door and sat down on the porch.

The air was chilly. Behind me, Slim waited for something to happen. He was getting cold. "Hurry up, I ain't going to stand here all night." Two minutes passed. I could hear him grumbling. "I thought you were sick."

Sick? Not me.

He sighed. "Okay, come back inside."

I scrambled through the open door and returned to my place on the floor. Drover was already there, the little...Slim chunked up the stove with a couple of pieces of hackberry, then walked through the house, looking for...well, a puddle or something. He found nothing. Hee hee.

"I'm going back to bed. I don't want to hear another squeak out of you owl-heads. Don't bark, don't snore, don't do anything, and stay out of the bathroom."

Yes sir.

He went back to his bedroom and turned off the light. I heard the squeak of his bedsprings, indicating that he had crawled back into the sack. What a grouch.

The house fell into a peaceful silence. Whew. I had dodged a bullet.

At that point, I turned a ferocious glare on my assistant. "Drover, do you have any idea what happened to me after you ran like a little chicken and left me alone in the bathroom?"

He lifted his head and gave me his usual silly grin. "Well, let me think. Did you get sick?"

"Yes. I got sick—because you sat there and let me drink two gallons of water laced with Babbo."

"I told you it tasted funny."

"It did NOT taste funny, it tasted horrible."

"Why'd you drink it?"

"Because...how dare you ask such a question?"

"Just curious, but I already know the answer."

"You *don't* know the answer. Even I can't figure it out. In certain respects...well, it wasn't the smartest thing I've ever done."

"You never listen. That's the answer."

I flinched. "What? Say that again, slowly."

"You. Never. Listen."

"That's ridiculous. I hear even the tiniest of sounds. My ears are high-tech instruments for gathering sounds."

"You *hear* but you don't *listen*. It's true. Go ahead and admit it."

"I will never admit such a pack of lies." In spite of myself, I gave his words some thought. "Drover, I'm willing to admit there might be a tiny grain of truth in what you say."

"More than that."

"All right, more than that. I admit it.

Sometimes…sometimes I don't listen. You're right."

He burst out laughing. "Hee hee hee. I can't believe you said that!"

"Please don't giggle when I've just made a confession."

"Sorry, I couldn't help it."

"Are you happy now?" He giggled and nodded. "Good. I hope you enjoyed your little moment of triumph, because now I must place you under arrest."

His jaw dropped three inches. "Arrest? What did I do?"

I rose from my spot on the floor and paced a few steps away. I could feel his gaze following me. "Drover, there's a fine line between honesty and treason, and you have crossed it."

"Yeah, but…" His grin wilted into an arc of concern. "Is this a joke?"

"I wish it were. No, it's not a joke. For weeks I've been observing this little rebellious streak of yours. Now it has broken out into the open and we must act."

"All I said was that you don't listen, and you even admitted I was right."

"I know, and the fact that it was true makes it twice as bad. On your feet, soldier. You will stand with your nose in the corner for two solid hours."

"Yeah, but..."

"March!"

"It's not fair!"

I gave him an escort to the northwest corner of the room and left him there with his nose in the appropriate spot. Then I returned to my place in front of the stove. He was whimpering and feeling sorry for himself. Tough toenails.

Okay, to be honest, I felt kind of bad about it. I hate to be severe with the men, but if I don't take a hard line, how will they learn Life's Lessons? When I took this job as Head of the Security Division, I didn't expect it to be easy, but I never thought...borp...

Excuse me. I never thought I would be drinking toilet cleaner. I mean, when you mix Babbo with popcorn, you come up with a bad combination. Fortunately, I had purged my system of the nasty stuff and all that remained were a few unpleasant memories. I was ready to go back to sleep.

I scratched around on the so-called carpet and prepared to do my Three Turns and Flop maneuver, when all at once, I noticed...well, there was a shadow on the wall. See, Slim had chunked up the stove, and now the room was illuminated by a glow of yellow light that came through the vent on the stove door. It threw an eerie shadow on the south wall.

I had seen it earlier and had assumed that it was my own shadow, but now…I wasn't so sure about that. I mean, the ears and nose…

I looked closer. The image seemed bigger than before. Good grief, unless I was badly mistaken, I was looking at the shadow of a BEAR!

Hey, I've never been the kind of dog that gets nervous about shadows, but this was something new and different, and scary enough to cause all the hairs on my back to stand at attention.

I found myself drifting over to Drover's prison cell. "Psst. Are you awake?"

"Snork murk snicklefritz."

"What?"

"Ticky tattle in the banana rodeo."

"You're asleep. I can always tell. Wake up."

I gave him a shake and his eyes slid open. "Gummy beans in beetle jeans. Where am I?"

"You're in prison. I've come to bail you out."

"Oh goodie. How come?"

"Because…Drover, I don't want to alarm you, but let's go right to the point. *I think we have a bear inside the house.*"

His eyes popped open. "A bear! Bears live in

the mountains."

"I agree, but remember what Slim said this morning? He said he saw a bear crossing the road."

"Yeah, but we decided it was a burro."

"I know, I know, but he mumbles his words sometimes and...what if he actually saw a bear? And what if it broke into the house?"

Drover's eyes grew as wide as full moons. "I wish you wouldn't say that."

"Drover, moments ago, I saw a big shadow on the wall and it sure looked like a bear. Look for yourself."

Very slowly, he moved his head around and squinted at the wall. "I don't see anything."

"Yes, well, they're sneaky. Maybe he's hiding somewhere. We need to post a double guard."

"You know, I think I'll stay in jail."

"You will *not* stay in jail! I need your help. Follow me." We crept out of the cell and made our way back to our sleeping quarters in front of the stove. There, we sat down. I swung my gaze around to the south wall and saw...oh no!

"Drover, look at the south wall and tell me what you see."

He turned his eyes toward the wall and let out a gasp. "Oh my gosh, two of them, and they're

huge!"

"Exactly, and now we come to the crucial question. Are they burros or bears?"

His voice came out as a terrified squeak. "Grizzly bears! How'd they get in the house?"

"I don't know, but they're here."

"What'll we do?"

My mind was racing. "Slim must be warned."

"Yeah, but we already woke him up once, and he threw a fit."

"I know, but this is a different deal. He needs to know that the house has been invaded." I pulled myself up to my full height. "Prepare to launch Stage Three Barking, and don't hold anything back."

"What if the bears come after us?"

I laid a paw upon his shoulder. "Then we'll go down fighting for the ranch. Ready? Commence firing!"

Boy, you talk about some spirited barking. We let fly with everything we had, and I have to give Drover credit. He didn't faint or hide under the coffee table or spin around in circles. He actually rallied to the cause and barked his little heart out. After thirty seconds of solid blasting, we got a response from the bedroom.

"SHUT UP!"

I wasn't surprised. That's always his first reaction to Code Threes in the middle of the night. We leaned into our work and barked louder than ever.

Again, Slim's voice came rolling down the hall. "If I have to get out of this bed, somebody's neck is liable to get wrung!"

The man wasn't totally rational when we had to wake him up, but, in our deepest hearts, we knew we were doing it for his own good.

At last we heard the squeak of bed springs, then the thunder of his hooves on the floor. His feet, actually. He had big feet but they weren't exactly hooves, and here they came. BOOM, BOOM, BOOM.

Seconds later, he stood right in front of us—stiff, disheveled, and fuming mad. "What are you morons barking at!"

Our noses pointed toward the terrifying scene on the wall—two enormous grizzly bears.

The moment of truth had arriven.

We Survive a
Dangerous Night

Okay, there we were. Slim turned and stared at the horrible scene on the wall. Drover and I held our breaths and waited for...I don't know, for him to grab a gun and start shooting, I suppose.

Hmmm. That was odd. The corners of his mouth began to curl upward and he said, "Is that what you're barking at?"

Well...yes, of course. Get the gun!

He uttered a grunt that sounded a bit like a chuckle. Yes, it was a chuckle, and it grew louder, turning into laughter. He staggered over to his big easy chair and flopped down, buried his face in his hands and moaned, "All I want to do is sleep. Is that asking too much?"

Drover and I exchanged glances. This was very strange.

He sat there for a moment, then uncovered his face and sat up straight. His smile dropped dead and his gaze slid around to...well, to me, it seemed. "Hank, I know it's hard to function in the normal world when you've got the brain of a grasshopper."

I...I didn't know how to respond to that, so I tapped my tail on the floor. Tap, tap, tap.

He went on. "I understand, I really do, but this has got to stop." He rose from the chair and walked over to the wall. He pointed to the bears. "These things are shadows of you and Stub Tail." He bent at the waist and drilled me with his eyes. *You're barking at your own shadows. Am I getting through?*

Huh? I narrowed my eyes and studied the... okay, maybe...hey, they had sure looked like bears to me, and Drover had thought so too.

"Quit barking at shadows. Quit barking at anything. Quit drinking out of the pot. It's four-o-dadgum-clock in the morning and you've woke me up twice. If it happens one more time, I'll become an angry, violent person. Your little tails will get kicked out that door yonder and you will spend the rest of the night in the cold, cruel world. Is there any part of this you don't understand?"

Gulp. Yes sir. Message received. I couldn't make any promises about Drover, but I would be as quiet as a little mouse.

Shaking his head and muttering under his breath, he went back to his bedroom. The storm had passed and we had survived.

I turned to Drover and saw that he was wearing a silly grin. "What are you grinning about?"

"We were barking at our own shadows. That's pretty funny."

"It's not funny at all."

"That's what I meant."

"The fact is, our sensing equipment gave us faulty information. We went into combat with a bogus report."

"Yeah, I sure got fooled." His grin vanished and he looked around with wide eyes. "Do you reckon it could happen again?"

"Oh no, not in a thousand years." There was a moment of silence. "Why do you ask?"

I noticed that he was doing something odd with his eyes, rolling them around and directing his gaze toward the...yipes...toward the south wall and two creepy, shadowy images.

I felt the hair rising on the back of my neck. "Drover, don't start this again. We don't have bears on this ranch."

"Yeah, but what about monsters?"

I swallowed hard and tried to conceal the quiver in my voice. "We do have monsters, hundreds of them. What are you suggesting?"

"I'm not sure. If we bark again, Slim'll throw us out of the house."

"Exactly, but if we don't bark...Drover, some of those monsters *eat dogs*."

"Yeah, I know. I'm getting a real bad feeling about this. Maybe we ought to hide."

My gaze swept the room, looking for a monster-proof bunker. "Yes, but where?"

"Under Slim's bed."

His words echoed through the corregidors of my mind, and just for a second, I had an uneasy thought: wasn't there some reason why we might not want to hide under the bed? Maybe so, but I couldn't think of it. You know how it is when you're under tremendous pressure.

"Under the bed, great idea. Quick, to the bunker!"

We went ripping down the hall and wiggled ourselves beneath the bed. Only then were we able to relax. I heard Drover's voice in the darkness. "We made it! We're safe."

"Yes, and I don't think the monsters followed us. Nice work, son. Now let's try to get some sleep." I took a big yawn, then...

"Hank?"

"What?"

"It stinks under here. And there's something wet."

"Wet?"

"Yeah, we're lying in it."

I sat up and noticed...huh?

Anyway, Drover and I talked it over and decided that...well, Slim wouldn't mind having two warm dogs in bed with him, and we felt that we would be happier too. It gets cold under those beds, don't you know, and you sure have to watch out for spiders.

That was the main thing. We were concerned about spiders. No kidding.

We were able to enter the bed without arousing Slim. That wasn't an accident. In the first place, he had fallen into a deep snoring sleep, but also we followed our Bed Entry Procedures to the letter: front paws on the bed, pull upward, back paws on the bed, and lie down at the feet of the host.

We had a few tense moments when our host

began talking in his sleep, but after a while, he quit and the operation turned out to be a huge success. Not only did we provide warmth and comfort to Slim's feet, but we slept better, knowing that we were safe from spiders. And from monsters and bears.

Anyway, we got a good night's sleep. About thirty minutes before daylight, we awoke and initiated the second phase of the procedure: Leave the Bed.

It's very important that we do the second phase, don't you see, because if we don't leave the bed in a stealthy manner...well, we get caught, and let's be honest. Our people don't necessarily rejoice when they find dogs in bed with them. Hencely, we've found that everyone is happier if we vanish before daylight.

On paws that made not a sound, we oozed ourselves off the bed and tiptoed back to the living room. By the time Slim came down the hall and greeted the day, we were curled up in front of the stove, two of the nicest, best-behavedest little doggies Texas had ever produced.

When Slim entered the living room, I sat up straight and gave him a bright Good Morning smile. He grunted something about "dogs barking all night," and went into the kitchen to start his coffee.

Whew. We had made it through another dark and dangerous night, and you know what? Slim never figured out what was causing that odd smell in his bedroom. Heh. He thought it came from his boots.

Well, after Slim drank his morning coffee, we loaded up in the pickup and prepared for another work day on the ranch. When we pulled into headquarters, we found Loper in front of the gas tanks, filling Sally May's car with gasoline. That seemed odd, because Loper rarely drove the car.

Odder still was the set of clothes he wore—not his usual jeans and a work shirt, but some strange costume with matching pants and jacket made of bright colored material. On his head, he wore a red knitted cap with a little puff of yarn on the top.

Slim looked him up and down. "Good honk, did you run out of clothes?"

"I don't want to hear about it."

"What is that?"

Loper forked him with a hostile glare. "It's a ski outfit. My wife bought it when I was looking the other way, and it wasn't cheap."

"It should have been. I wouldn't even wear it on a dark night."

"Well, you have no taste in fashion. And you have no wife. If you ever get one, you'll spend the first six months eating your own words. I'll be glad to furnish the salt and pepper."

A nasty little smirk slithered across Slim's mouth. "Does this mean you're fixing to go on a ski trip?"

"What do you think? A group from the church is going to Glorieta. I fought it for three months." He glanced at his watch. "We should have left thirty minutes ago."

"You'll have a great time, I know you will."

"I will NOT have a great time. I'll spend every minute thinking about my banker."

"Is he going?"

"No, he's too cheap. He'll be sitting in his office, looking at my loan papers."

"Oh, good. A man wouldn't want his banker to see him wearing..." Slim snorted a laugh and turned away. "...*that*."

Loper's face had turned a dangerous shade of red. "You go right ahead and laugh all you want, mister. We'll be gone three days and you'll have the whole ranch to take care of, and the weather report says a big cold front is heading this way."

"I can handle it."

"You'll have to chop ice on all the stock tanks."

"I can handle it."

"Make sure the plumbing doesn't freeze in your house. Throw out some grain for the wild turkeys. Give the cattle plenty of feed, but not too much. That feed's gotten higher than a cat's back."

Slim gave his head a shake. "Give the cattle plenty of feed, but not too much. That's about as clear as mud."

"Well, maybe you can figure it out. The main thing is, try not to do anything stupid while I'm gone. Any questions?"

Slim slouched against the side of the car. "Are you actually going to get on skis? Last time I checked, you had trouble walking on your own feet."

"They give lessons. I'll do whatever I have to do to keep the peace."

"Well, you look real cute, and you'll look even cuter on crutches." Slim chuckled at his own humor. Loper remained stone-faced. "Oh, quit being such a grouch. You might as well try to act human for a few days. You might even surprise yourself and have fun. I know you're against fun, but you ought to try it."

Loper gazed off into the distance and shook his head. "You just blow like the wind. What do you know about fun?"

"Well, I've read about it in the magazines, and one of these days, I'm going to try it myself."

"Bachelors. Your life is so simple. Well, like it or not, I'm going to the slopes with a wife and two kids. When we leave, walk through the house and make sure everything's turned off and okay."

Loper had forgotten about his main job, filling the gas tank, and you'll never guess what happened next. Keep reading.

CHAPTER SIX

I Trick the Cat,
Hee Hee

Here's what happened. The tank filled up and gasoline splashed out on Loper's hand. Slim said, "Tank's full."

"Thanks." He hung the nozzle on a loop of baling wire and looked at his hand, which had been pretty thoroughly splattered. He glanced around. "Here, dogs. Hank, come here!"

Huh?

I had been sitting nearby, and by the time I figured out what had happened, it was too late to run for cover. Drover, on the other hand, had somehow...I don't know how the little slacker always disappears when it's time for the cowboys to wipe a dipstick or clean their hands, but he does, and we're talking about POOF, gone without a trace.

So, once again, I had been called up for service to the ranch. I squared my shoulders and moved closer to the boss, and soon became his grease rag. He mopped his hands on my back and sides, then scrubbed his fingernails on my ears.

What did I get out of it? A pat on the ribs and, "Thanks, pooch, you do good work."

Yeah, right, and for the next thirty minutes, I would have to do Dives in the Grass to get rid of the stench.

Loper started back to the house. "Oh, and feed the cat. I'll call you tonight to check on things. Good luck."

"Don't call me tonight. You won't have anything to say and neither will I. Everything's going to be fine. I know you think this ranch falls apart every time you leave, but you'd be surprised how well things work when we get you off the place." Just as Loper went through the yard gate, Slim cupped a hand around his mouth and yelled, "Oh, by the way, yesterday morning, I saw a bear in the road."

Over his shoulder, Loper yelled back, "Don't drink on company time," and went into the house.

Slim grinned and shook his head. "Boy, that man's got a thick skull, and I think he needs a hearing aid too."

He seemed to be speaking to me, as though I might have had some interest in their conversation. I didn't. I was still preoccupied with rubbing the gasoline stench off my coat.

Slim drifted down to the corrals and began his morning chores. He fed the horses, checked some yearlings in the sick pen, and threw out some grain for the wild turkeys. Loper and Sally May finally got their luggage and children loaded in the car, and left in a cloud of dust.

When they'd gone, Slim and I walked down to the house. Before going inside to make sure Sally May had turned off all the appliances and hadn't left any water running, Slim put out a bowl of Kitty Krumbles for Sally May's little sneak of a cat. He set the bowl on the porch and went inside to do his walk-around of the house.

When the door closed behind him, I realized that...well, Sally May and her broom were on their way to Glorieta, and nobody was watching the yard, the cat, or me.

Guess what naughty thoughts entered my mind. Hee hee.

I dived over the fence and went creeping toward the porch. Pete was already there, of course, gobbling and slobbering over the Kitty

Krumbles—a brand of cat food that was about five-times better than he deserved. In fact, it was the most expensive brand on the market.

You think this world isn't in sad shape? The cat does *nothing* around here and gets high-dollar, tuna-flavored tidbits shaped like stars and donuts. We dogs put in eighteen hours a day and work ourselves into the ground, and we get Co-op dog food, hard lumps of something that has the flavor of wood shavings.

Do you know why they give the cat high-dollar food? Because he won't eat the cheap stuff, and apparently somebody cares. If I'd been in charge, I would have bought the cheapest ration money could buy, and told him to eat it or go hungry. But nobody around here listens to the dogs.

Anyway, kitty was "dining," shall we say, when I rolled up to the porch. He lifted his gaze and gave me his usual insolent smirk. "My goodness, it's Hankie the Wonderdog. Let me guess: you're here to ask if I saw the bear."

I stared into his scheming little eyes. "What bear?"

"Slim saw a bear on the road."

"Oh, that. Yes, I know all about it. He didn't see a bear, he saw a burro, a donkey. We don't have bears on this ranch."

Pete rolled his eyes around. "What would you say if I told you I saw him too?"

"I would say that you're up to your usual tricks. I would laugh in your face."

"I saw the bear, Hankie. He walked through headquarters at daylight this morning."

"No kidding? In that case," I stuck my nose right in his face and pressed the Ha Ha Button. "Ha ha ha ha ha!"

Pete hated that. He flatted his ears and beamed me a smoldering glare. "Very well, Hankie, you've been warned."

"Thanks for the warning, and here's one for you. Back away from the bowl. I need to run some tests on your food."

The cat glared and twitched the end of his tail. "Hankie, if you want a bite, I'm willing to share."

"Share? Ha ha. Sorry, Pete, but sharing with cats isn't something we do on this outfit. Go chase your tail."

He backed away from the bowl. "It's not as good as you think."

"It'll be better than I think, and do you know why? Because I'm stealing it from you. Buzz off."

Heh heh. I got him told, didn't I? You bet, and it was true, every word of it. The best food in this world is what you can conflagrate from a greedy little ranch cat. Confiscate.

Pete vanished and I went to work on his Kitty Krumbles. Great stuff, nice and crunchy, with the delicate flavor of broiled tuna. I had crunched my way through several mouthfuls when I heard a voice behind me: Drover. He was standing at the yard gate.

"Oh, hi. Can I have some cat food?"

"No."

"Drat. Is it pretty good?"

"It's excellent, delicious. It's a crime to waste it on a cat."

"I'll be derned. That's what Pete said about our dog food."

My head came up and I stopped chewing. "He's eating our dog food?"

"Yep, he's up at the machine shed right now."

"Good. Nobody deserves Co-op more than Pete."

"Yeah, but he loves it. He says it's too good to waste on dogs."

I marched over to the gate. "Let me get this straight. Pete is eating *our* food, and loves it, and you stood there and watched him eat?"

"I didn't figure you'd care."

"What ever gave you that idea?"

"Well, you're always complaining about it."

"Drover, food isn't the issue here. We're talking about Ranch Rules. Cats are not allowed to mooch our dog food, period."

"Yeah, but..."

I leaped over the fence. "Never mind, I'll handle it."

"Can I have some cat food?"

"Sure, help yourself. It tastes like dead fish."

Drover hopped over the fence and scampered to the bowl of cat food on the porch. I stormed up the hill and rumbled over to the cat. "Okay, Pete, this has gone far enough. Hands up, back away from the bowl."

"But Hankie..."

"Move!"

He backed away from the bowl. "Hankie, I'm confused. First, you wanted my cat food, and now you want your dog food."

"Well, you got one thing right, kitty: you're confused."

"Shall I go back to my cat food? Will that make you happy?"

"When you vanish, I'll be happy."

Pete heaved a loud sigh. "Well, I guess I'll go back to my pitiful bowl of cat food."

"You do that, and the next time I catch you stealing dog food, you won't get off so easy. Scram."

Kitty scrammed and I took a bite of good honest American dog food, which had no hint of fishy taste. Okay, sometimes it reminded me of wood shavings and sawdust, but give me sawdust any day over dead fish. Co-op isn't dainty, just

61

solid and honest, like the dogs who eat it.

I was crunching a delicious bite of Co-op when Drover came up the hill, huffing and puffing. "Hank, you said I could eat the cat food, right? Well, Pete came back and said it was his, and wouldn't let me eat any more."

"So what? Let the little crook have all he wants. The important thing is that he would rather be eating our dog food, but he can't. It's forbidden."

"You know, I think he got what he wanted."

That grabbed my attention. "What is that supposed to mean?"

"Well, he's laughing his head off, 'cause he tricked you into eating your own food."

I went nose-to-nose with the runt. "He didn't trick me. I tricked him."

"What was the trick?"

"The trick was..." I turned my gaze toward the house. Pete was sitting on the porch, gobbling cat food. He saw me, grinned, and waved a paw. I spit the last of the Co-op out of my mouth. "This stuff tastes like peanut shells."

"Yeah, that's what he said."

"Stop telling me what he said. Drover, it's becoming clear that we've been conned by the cat."

"*You* were."

"What?"

"I said...what a crooked little cat."

"Exactly my point. He used slimy, underhanded tricks to...to do something." I rose to my full height and rolled the muscles in my massive shoulders. "And he's fixing to get a painful education. Let's go down there and teach him some manners."

"Oh, I think I'll stay here. I'm kind of hungry."

I gave him a scorching glare. "The Security Division has been sandbagged by the cat...and you're hungry? What kind of dog are you?"

"Oh, the kind that gets hungry, I guess."

"Fine. Stay here and eat slop, but I'm warning you, this will go into my report."

"Works for me."

"I beg your pardon?"

"I said...go git 'im, Hankie, beat him up!"

"Thanks. That's exactly what I have in mind."

I turned my nose toward the house and hit the ignition button on Engines One and Two. Moments later, I was roaring down the hill. The cat would pay a terrible price for his treachery.

I didn't even pause at the fence, but went flying over...BAM...okay, our instruments gave us a faulty reading about the height of the fence, but those things happen in the heat of combat.

The important thing is that I'm no quitter. I picked myself off the ground, went soaring over the fence, and rushed to the porch, where I had every intention of wrecking the...hmmm, the cat had vanished, which was fine. Wrecking the cat would have been fun, but my main objective was to recapture his...huh?

The cat food was gone!

CHAPTER SEVEN

Slim Gets Stopped By the Police

The little creep had gobbled down every morsel of the Kitty Krumbles, leaving nothing but the lingering fragrance of tuna. I rushed back to the machine shed.

"Drover, we've had a change of plans. Scoot over, we're going to share the Co-op." I shoved the runt out of the way and prepared to...the hub cap was empty, and Drover was licking crumbs off his chops. "Greedy pig, you ate it all!"

"Well, you said it was slop."

"Of course it's slop, but it's *our* slop. I'm surrounded by thieves and gluttons."

"Yeah, but..."

"Go to your room...immediately!"

Drover went slinking away and I roared back

down to the yard to settle accounts with the cat. I found him, perched on a limb of a big hackberry tree. I rushed to the base of the tree and blasted him with Barks of Outrage. "Pete, you're despicable!"

He licked his paw and smirked down at me. "I know, Hankie, and sometimes it really bothers me. But the question is, did you learn anything from this experience?"

"Of course I did. Cats cheat."

He smirked and fluttered his eyelids. "Well, yes, Hankie, sometimes we're forced to bend the rules, but that's not the lesson I'm talking about."

"I don't care about your so-called lessons. I don't take lessons from cats."

"I know you don't, but listen anyway." He leaned out on the limb and lowered his voice. *"Be content with what you have. Stop wanting what isn't yours.* Oh, and you'd better watch out for that bear."

Here's the good part. The little fraud had gotten so caught up in giving me his silly advice, he leaned too far out on the limb and fell out of the tree. Ho! As you can imagine, I pounced on this opportunity, chased him around the yard, and ran him up another tree.

Glaring up at him, I beamed a triumphant

smile. "That's what I think of your lessons, you little hickocrip, and now I'm going to teach *you* a lesson. Since you hogged all the food, I'm going to *chew up your food bowl!*"

His eyes widened. "Really! You'd actually do that?"

"You bet your boots I would. When I get done, your food bowl will be smithereens."

He chirped a little laugh. "Hankie, you're a piece of work."

"You'd better believe it, kitty. The mind of a dog is an awesome thing."

Heh heh. Did I get him told or what?

I marched over to the porch and swept up the plastic bowl in my enormous jaws. Then, while the scheming little cat watched with horror-stricken eyes, I proceeded to crunch up his food bowl. I had every intention of reducing it to tiny splinters and particles, only...

Huh? The door opened and out stepped Slim. He saw me there on the porch and seemed...well, surprised.

"What are you doing?"

I was...see, the cat had tricked me into...and then Drover...all at once, I was overwhelmed by the thought that this looked...fairly ridiculous.

Slim snatched the bowl out of my mouth. He

examined what was left of it and gave his head a shake. "Meathead. You're supposed to eat the food, not the bowl."

Yes, but...

"Quit eating plastic bowls and get out of the yard. Scat!"

Yes sir.

"Try to act your age, not your IQ."

Boy, that hurt. Make one little mistake around here and they hang it around your neck and let you wear it for the next six...although I wouldn't say that it was exactly a mistake. Don't forget that in the Larger Scheme of Things, I had won a moral victory over the cat.

He got the food, but I wrecked his bowl. It was a huge moral victory.

Anyway, Slim drove to the feed barn and loaded twenty sacks of feed into the bed of the pickup. He whistled for us dogs to load up and off we went to feed cattle. I probably should have insisted that Drover spend the rest of the day, standing with his nose in the corner, but...oh well.

Off we went, driving down the county road, a cowboy and his two loyal dogs, when, suddenly, out of nowhere, we heard the shriek of...what was that? It was a high-pitched, shrill sound, louder than the squeal of a loose fan belt. Slim scowled and glanced at me, so I...well, I barked. That's what we do when we're not sure what's going on. We bark first and ask questions later.

Slim glanced in his rear-view mirror and saw flashing lights. We had been overtaken by a police cruiser—on an empty dirt road, twenty-five miles out in the country.

He pulled over to the side of the road and growled, "Don't they have any crooks to chase?"

An officer walked up to Slim's open window. I recognized him and so did Slim: Chief Deputy Bobby Kile. Slim began to relax. "Oh, it's you. Morning, Bobby."

"Morning, Slim." He was writing on his ticket book and he looked pretty serious about it. "I clocked you at seventy-five miles an hour."

Slim snorted a laugh. "This thing wouldn't go seventy-five if it was falling off a cliff."

"Driver's license?"

"I don't carry it when I'm working on the ranch."

The deputy nodded and wrote that down. He glanced at the safety inspection sticker on the windshield. "That expired two years ago."

"This is the feed truck. We don't drive it off the ranch."

"Uh huh." The deputy looked inside the cab. "No infant seat for the little dog, no seat belt for the big dog, and you're not wearing a safety helmet." He wrote it down and looked under the pickup. "Unsafe exhaust system."

"Bobby, you ain't funny."

The deputy wrote some more. "Mouthing off to an officer of the law. Where do you want your mail sent while you're in prison?"

I was stunned. Prison! Holy smokes, who would feed the dogs while he was...

Wait, hold everything. Never mind. It was all a big joke and they broke out laughing.

"Bobby, you're giving the sheriff's department a bad name. What are you doing out here in the Wild West?"

"Investigating an accident, happened yesterday morning. A pickup pulling a stock trailer went into the ditch and landed on its side. The driver swerved to miss a deer."

"Good honk. Was anybody hurt?"

"Nope. He walked to the Barnett place and they gave him a ride into town."

"Oh, good."

"He was hauling a bear. It took off and we can't find it."

There was a long moment of silence. Then

Slim said, "Did you say he was hauling a *bear?*"

"Ten-four, a black bear, half-grown."

Slim whistled under his breath and pushed his hat to the back of his head. "I saw him yesterday morning, only I thought I was losing my mind. But why would a man be driving through this country, hauling a bear?"

"He's a game ranger from New Mexico. The bear was hanging around a ranch north of Clayton, so they trapped him. The ranger was taking him to a zoo in Oklahoma City."

"The bear was 'hanging around a ranch?' What does that mean?"

"He tore the door off the saddle shed and ate a hundred pounds of sweet feed. The rancher was a little concerned that he might come into the house for breakfast." The deputy looked up at the sky. "We've got a problem."

"I guess we do. What do you suggest?"

The deputy shrugged. "Keep your eyes open. Use common sense, if you've got any. Pay attention to your dogs. They'll be the first to know if the bear's around."

Slim chuckled and glanced at...why was he looking at ME? "I'm glad you have so much faith in my dogs. They woke me up at four o'clock this morning, barking at their own shadows."

"Well, good luck. I'm going to alert all your neighbors. If you see the bear or find tracks, give me a call." The deputy's face grew solemn. "Slim, I'm going to let you off with a warning this time, but those dogs need to be wearing a seat belt."

They parted with a round of laughter. Deputy Kile blew his siren again and went on his way. Slim's laughter faded out. "Dogs, there's a bear running around our neighborhood, and we need to find him before he finds us." He leaned toward me until our noses were almost touching. "Are you listening?"

Maybe it wasn't the best time for me to lick him on the nose, but sometimes we get these sudden impulses, don't you see, and...well, my tongue leaped out and mopped his nose. I think it surprised him. He jerked backward, wiped his mouth with the back of his hand, and spit out the window.

"That's what I thought. I'm talking to chunk of firewood."

Well, gee, he didn't need to get all huffy about it. I mean, we dogs don't go around licking people we don't care about. When we lick 'em, it means... chunk of firewood. Boy, they really know how to hurt a dog.

Slim put the pickup in gear and started on

down the road. I whirled around to Drover. For once, he had been listening, and his eyes had grown as wide as plates. "Donkey Hoety, huh? Did you hear what the deputy just said?"

"Yeah, but I'm hoping it was a joke."

"The only joke around here is us, the ranch's Security Division. We got the Bear Report yesterday, and you botched it so badly, we were looking for donkeys and strawberries!"

"Well, you said…"

I stuck my nose in his face. "We look pathetic! Burros, berries, shadows on the wall…Drover, someone who didn't know better might think we're just a couple of dumb dogs."

"You really think so?"

"Yes, and you know what? I'm beginning to wonder about that myself."

The little mutt was almost in tears. "Now I'm all discouraged. What's left of life if we're just a couple of dumb dogs? Where do we go from here?"

His questions plunged us into a cloud of gloom, as each of us looked inward for some glimmer of hope. Did we find it? You'll have to keep reading.

CHAPTER EIGHT

I Encounter a Couple of Buzzards

The Security Division had been plunged into a time of great darkness. At last, I spoke. "Soldier, we've got to learn from our mistakes and make a fresh start. The first thing we'll do is destroy all the Wandering Donkey files. If someone in this office messed up, the world doesn't need to know about it."

"Gosh, you mean..."

"Yes. The case doesn't exist. If anyone asks about Donkey Hoety, we never heard of him. Our second course of action—and this will have a tremendous positive effect on morale—our second course of action will be..." I looked my assistant straight in the eyes. "Drover, I think we can blame this whole shameful episode on the cat."

He stared at me for a moment, then a tiny ray of sunshine broke through the clouds of his fog. "Gosh, no fooling?"

"Yes. Look at the evidence. Number one, the cat saw a bear this morning and didn't tell us."

"How'd you know that?"

"He told me."

"Oh. That makes sense."

"Exactly. Number two, we have reason to suspect that Pete planted garbage bombs in our data systems. It caused just enough damage to throw us off the chase and send us down a blind alley. In other words, we can blame it all on the cat."

His grin spread from ear to shining sea. "You know, I'm starting to feel better. But what about the bear?"

I took a deep breath and gazed out the window. "The bear remains a problem. We'll just hope he doesn't show up."

"I hear that. I'm scared of bears. Are you?"

His question caught me off guard and it took me a moment to think of an answer. "I've never seen one, Drover. When I do, I'll let you know."

That seemed to ease his mind, but it didn't make me feel any better. *Of course I was scared of bears!* I'd never seen one, but I didn't need to see one. They're huge. They have long teeth, powerful jaws, and claws that can gut a deer.

Any dog in his right mind is scared of bears, but the Head of Ranch Security can't go around blabbing about all the things he's scared of. If we did, what would happen to the Drovers of the world? They'd fall to pieces, and then what would we do?

Part of being brave is pretending that you really are—and hoping you'll never have to prove it.

Once we had cleared the air and pinned all the blame on Pete, we went on about our feeding chores. This time, Drover and I kept a sharp eye out for bears, not for donkeys or burros, but the result was pretty muchly the same. We saw nothing out of the ordinary.

The only excitement of the day came when Slim turned on the radio to listen to the weather report. If you recall, the ranch's feed truck had a special radio antenna. Years ago, the original one had been amputated by a bale of hay that slid off the top of a load, and Slim had "fixed it" by wiring a metal clothes hanger to the stub. It worked sometimes, but to get decent reception, you had to drive to a high spot in the pasture.

That's what we did, and there we heard: "...

Winter Storm Advisory for the Texas and Oklahoma Panhandles: falling temperatures, high winds, and wind chills in the range of twenty to thirty degrees below zero."

Slim's eyebrows jumped. "Good honk, it's fifty degrees right now, and they're talking about thirty below zero? That's serious cold. We'd better wind this up and cut some stove wood."

Right. We sure didn't need any frozen dogs in the living room.

We hurried through the rest of the feeding routine and picked up the chainsaw at the barn. We drove down along the creek and located several dead hackberry and chinaberry trees that we could harvest for stove wood. Slim went to work, buzzing his way through tree limbs and loading chunks of firewood into the back of the pickup.

The weather that afternoon was so warm and soft, Slim stripped down to his tee shirt and had to stop several times to wipe the sweat off his forehead. It made you wonder if the guys at the Weather Bureau knew what they were talking about.

While Slim ran the chainsaw, I sneezed the opportunity to do a little scouting. I mean, those of us in the Security Division had worked our way through the Donkey Disaster and we now had reliable information that a bear—an actual, living bear—had escaped on or near our ranch. It was time for us to get on the case and do some serious investigating.

I went down to the creek and worked the north bank, sniffing for unusual scents and checking for tracks in the mud. I'd never seen a bear track before, but had reason to suppose that I would recognize one if I saw it. How? Huge. If I ran across the biggest track I'd ever seen in my life, I would be pretty sure that it belonged to the bear.

I found scent and plenty of tracks, but they were just what you would expect: wild turkey, cottontail rabbit, deer, and raccoon. I kept working my way east down the creek, and all of a sudden... there it was, a set of tracks so big, they *had* to have been made by a bear.

A tingle of fear scampered down my backbone, and at that same moment, I thought I heard voices. I cocked my left ear and listened. Sure enough...

"P-p-a?"

"What."

"Are you a-a-asleep, asleep?"

"What do you think?"

"W-well, I w-w-wasn't s-sure and thought I'd ch-check."

"I was taking a nap till you woke me up to ask if I was asleep."

"Oh. S-s-sorry."

"No you ain't. If you was truly sorry, you wouldn't have woke me up in the first place."

"I g-g-guess you're r-r-right. G-go on and h-have a g-g-good n-nap."

"Junior, you've already ruined my nap by waking me up, so why'd you wake me up?"

"W-w-w-well, I j-j-just have a f-feeling the w-w-weather's gonna change. It's t-too w-w-warm for this t-t-time of year."

"Son, the weather's always a-changing. It's warm, it's cold. Today it's warm, so don't complain. It could be worse."

"Yeah, that's w-w-what b-bothers me. The other b-buzzards f-f-flew s-south and w-w-we're still h-h-here, still here."

Have you figured out who belonged to those voices? Here's a hint: two big black birds, one named "Junior" and the other going under the name of "Pa."

I had just stumbled into a conversation between Wallace and Junior, the buzzards.

I crept forward until I found myself standing

at the base of a big cottonwood tree. There, I lifted both Earatory Scanners and continued monitoring their conversation.

"Junior, the other buzzards went south and we missed the train. There ain't one thing I can do about it."

"Y-yeah, b-b-but I t-told you they were l-l-leaving."

"That's right, and what did I tell you?"

"W-w-well…"

"I told you I had a belly ache. When was the last time you tried flying six hundred miles on a sour stomach?"

"Y-y-yeah, c-c-cause you ate that whole s-s-skunk, whole skunk."

"Did not!"

"D-d-did t-t-too, did too."

"Junior, you tell the biggest whoppers! I gave you a whole leg to eat."

"Y-y-you gave m-me a f-f-foot."

"Well…he had big feet. There was a lot of good meat on that foot."

"Y-y-yeah, but y-you ate m-m-more than y-your share. Y-you've got n-n-no more t-t-table m-manners than a g-g-goat."

"Well? What do you expect? We're buzzards, son. We ain't hummingbirds or cedar wrens.

When the dinner bell rings, a buzzard needs to make his move."

"I'm h-h-hungry, and w-we ought to b-b-be d-down south with the r-r-rest of the b-buzzards."

"Well, we ain't down south. Am I going to have to listen to you whine all winter long?"

"P-p-pa?"

"What!"

"There's a d-d-dog at the b-b-base of our t-t-tree, our tree."

Wallace hadn't noticed me, but now he craned his long skinny neck and looked down. "That ain't a dog, it's a...I don't know what it is, but it sure has an ugly nose."

"It's our d-d-doggie f-f-friend."

Wallace squinted his eyes. "Why, it is a dog, sure 'nuff." He licked his beak and flashed a wicked buzzardly grin. "Reckon he'd eat? I've about gone through that skunk and my belly bones are starting to rattle."

"W-w-well, he ain't d-d-dead, ain't dead, P-p-pa."

"Junior, I think he's dead. He don't look smart enough to be alive."

"I'll a-a-ask him." Junior turned a pleasant smile on me. "H-hi, d-d-doggie. M-me and my p-p-pa were w-w-wondering...are y-you d-d-dead y-y-yet?"

Oh brother. What do you say to a couple of buzzards who wonder if you're dead yet? Well, you can get mad or you can have a little fun. I decided on the fun. "Why yes, I am. What can I do for you?"

They traded long glances, and Wallace spoke in a whisper. "Be careful, son, there's something about this that don't add up."

"Y-y-you mean..."

"I think he's lying. Let me handle this." Wallace looked down at me and held up one foot. "Dog, how many claws am I a-holding up?"

"Seventeen."

Wallace turned back to Junior. "That's the wrong answer."

"Y-yeah, and he-he ain't d-d-dead."

"Let me try another one. Dog, how long is a piece of string?"

"Thirty-two."

That sent them back into another huddle. Wallace drew circles in the air beside his head. "Something's wrong with that dog, and I'm a-thinking he's still alive."

We'd gotten off to a slow start, but it appeared that we were making some progress. It was time for me to launch into a serious interrogation of the buzzards.

CHAPTER NINE

Buzzard Music

Junior said, "S-s-s-ee? I t-t-told you h-he w-w-wasn't d-d-dead."

"You did not tell me no such thing. All you said was…" Wallace whipped his head around to me. "Dog, you don't need to go around acting like a smarty-pants."

I couldn't hold back a chuckle. "Wallace, when you ask ridiculous questions, you get ridiculous answers."

"Puppy dog, there's nothing ridiculous about supper. That's what buzzards do. We're in the supper business."

"Yeah? How's business?"

"Business is awful, down thirty-one percent."

"Sorry to hear that."

"No you ain't. If you really gave a rip, you wouldn't be wearing that grin all over your face."

I laughed. "You tagged me there. I really don't give a rip, so let's talk about something else. I'm doing a patrol of ranch property and I need to know if you've seen anything suspicious."

A sly grin spread across Wallace's beak. "Well, now, as a matter of fact, yes, only I ain't going to tell you about it." He winked at Junior. "Teach him to be a smarty-pants, heh."

"Oh g-g-go ahead and t-t-tell him, P-p-pa. He's the g-g-guard dog and h-h-he needs to know."

"Why? He wouldn't believe me if I told him."

"W-w-well, t-tell him anyway, anyway."

Wallace pulled on his chin and cut his eyes from side to side. "All right, but we'll make him guess. There's no way he'll get it right." He gave Junior a wink and turned back to me. "Okay, puppy, this morning at daylight, me and Junior seen something very, very suspicious, and there's no way you'll ever guess the right answer."

"What if I do?"

"Well, you won't. I guarantee you'll never think of this, not in a thousand years."

"But if I do? Here's an idea. If, by some miracle, I get the right answer, you have to say 'Thank You' fifty times."

See, I knew old Wallace hated manners and being polite. Junior had been working on him for years, trying to improve his social skills, but the old coot had resisted every attempt to teach him manners.

Junior loved my idea and broke into a big grin. "Oh, th-that's w-w-wicked!"

"Junior, hush, I'm a-trying to think." Wallace paced back and forth on the limb, scowling and pulling on his chin. "All right, doggie, we'll do the deal, but here's the other side. If you lose, which you will, you have to say 'Buzzards is beautiful' sixty times."

"You're on, we've got a bet."

Wallace grinned at Junior. "Son, I've got this one in the sack."

Heh. I had a feeling that I knew the answer, and that old Wallace was fixing to get the shock of his life.

He was looking very smug about this, and said, "All right, dog, go ahead and make your guess, and be prepared to lose."

I paused for a moment to add a little drama to the presentation, then looked up the tree and said, "You saw a half-grown black bear. He crossed the creek and walked right past your tree."

Wallace looked as though he'd backed into an

electric fence. His eyes bugged out and I thought he might fall out of the tree. It was hilarious, one of the funniest moments of my whole career. We're talking about shocked beyond description.

He puffed himself up to his full height, whipped around to Junior, and yelled, "This is the rottenest dirty deal I ever saw! Who told him that?"

"N-not me, P-pa, honest."

"You had to tell him! There's no way..." He jerked his head around and scorched me with a pair of flaming eyes. "You cheated, dog! I don't know how you done it, but you're a low-down cheater and a rotten egg eater!"

I cackled out loud. "I didn't cheat, Wallace, and Junior didn't tell me. Let's just say I got lucky."

"Lucky my foot! You're as crooked as a snake."

"Too bad. You lost, so pay off."

"I ain't going to pay off! It was rigged."

Junior nodded. "H-he's r-right, P-pa, y-y-you lost. P-p-play fair."

"Play fair! What kind of buzzard are you?"

Junior laid a wing across his shoulder. "P-pa, it w-w-won't h-hurt for l-long."

Wallace shoved him away. "Don't touch me! You have no idea how bad it's going to hurt. I'd rather sit on a cactus bush than say thank you!" Boy, you talk about steamed. That was one mad buzzard. "All right, puppy, I'll pay off. What would you think if I made it into a song?"

"I'd hate it. I've heard you sing before, and to be real honest, it shattered my nerves."

A big smirk bloomed on his beak. "Too bad. Hang onto your drawers, 'cause you're fixing to get shattered."

And with that, he launched himself into his Thank You Song.

Thank You

You cheated me with sneaky tricks, and now I
    have to pay.
You're making me repeat two words I rarely
    ever say.
We made a bet. You won, I lost, so listen for a
    while.
And here's your fifty thank-yous, delivered
    buzzard-style.

Thank you, thank you, I wish that I could
    spank you.
Thank you!
Thank you!
Thank you, thank you, thank you!

You want some more? Well, listen here:
Thank you, thank you, thank you.

Thank you, thank you, thank you, pooch,
and stick 'em in your ear.

In case you thought your little trick would
make me more polite,
This solemn presentation should set the record
right.
If you're too dumb to get the point, again I'll
have to say:
I'll be a buzzard, unrepentant, 'til my dying day.

Thank you, thank you, I wish that I could
spank you.
Thank you!
Thank you!
Thank you, thank you, thank you!

You want some more? Well, listen here:
Thank you, thank you, thank you.
Thank you, thank you, thank you, pooch,
and stick 'em in your ear.

I'm proud to be a buzzard, I'm proud to be
uncouth.
I despise all forms of manners and that's the
gospel truth.
The trouble is that saying "thank you" always

makes me sick,
And throwing up on mouthy dogs is a famous
　　buzzard trick. Ha!

Thank you, thank you, I think that I shall
　　tank you.
Thank you!
Thank you!
Thank you, thank you, thank you!

You ever see a buzzard launch his dinner
　　from a tree?
Thank you, thank you, thank you, pooch,
And here's a gift from me!

Sometimes, during presentations of buzzard music, my mind wanders. I mean, it's so bad, the mind wishes to fly away to a happier place. But on this occasion, I just happened to be listening to his words, and caught just enough to realize that trouble was heading my way.

See, the old sneak had devised a way of getting his revenge. When he sang that line about pitching his lunch from a tree, he wasn't kidding. That's what buzzards do when they're mad or unhappy: they throw up on whoever made 'em that way. And we don't need to go into horrifying details about what buzzards eat.

Bottom line: you don't want to get hit.

When he launched, I saw it coming and had just enough time to scramble out of the way. The awful stuff hit the ground with a splat, and fellers, you talk about STINK! I'm sure it killed every weed and blade of grass within fifty feet.

I beamed him a glare. "Now, why'd you have to go and do that?"

"By grabbies, you made me do manners and it made me ill, and that's what you get—paybacks! Teach you to force manners on a buzzard. I hope you get corns on your feet and fleas in your hair."

"Yeah, well, I kept a count on your thank-yous, and you only did thirty-eight. You owe me twelve more."

His eyes lit up. "Well, now, that ain't a problem. If you want to get all huffy about it, I'll sing that song again, fifty times, if you want. Hee. To be real honest, I'd love to take another shot at you, even if it means saying a bunch of mealy-mouth thank yous."

I backed farther away from the tree, just in case he was reloading. "No, that's okay. You cheated, but I'm not going to press my luck."

He gave a snarling laugh. "Well, maybe you ain't as dumb as you look. Sorry you have to leave so soon. Have a nice day. Or, even better, go sit on a porcupine and come back sometime when you can't stay so long."

"Thanks, Wallace, it's always a pleasure doing business with you. See you around, Junior, and watch out for bears."

I returned to the pickup, chuckling to myself and enjoying the memory of old Wallace yelling "Thank You!" It had really made my day...but then a darker thought moved across my mind. A black bear was running loose on our ranch, and you know what? That wasn't so funny.

I slowed to a walk and noticed something else that wasn't funny. The air, which had been soft and still all afternoon, had begun to stir...and it was cold—not just cool or chilly, but *cold*. We're talking about air from a deep freeze. Dark clouds raced over us from the north, and all at once, tumbleweeds began loping south across the prairie.

Slim noticed it too. He had stripped down to his tee shirt, you might recall, and now he felt the sudden chill. He looked up at the sky and that's when the wind slammed us—a blast of frigid air that turned his breath into fog.

"Load up, dogs! Let's get out of here."

By the time we made it back to Slim's place, the wind was screaming through the big cottonwood trees along the creek. I don't know how much the temperature had dropped, but it was falling like a cinder block, and little bullets of ice smacked our faces as we ran to the house.

We darted inside and Slim went to work stoking up the fire. Nice idea, but the wind was coming down the stove pipe and pushed clouds of smoke into the house. See, when the fire in your stove burns down to ashes, there isn't enough heat going up the chimney to keep the cold air from coming down.

Slim had been through this before and knew what to do. He built a roaring fire with newspaper and got the stove hot enough so that the chimney would draw, then he added pieces of pine lumber and small chunks of hackberry bark, until he had a good hot fire and was able to close the stove door.

He heaved a sigh and fanned the smoke away from his face. "Dogs, we're in for a bad night."

He had no idea how true those words would turn out to be. Neither did I, but I was getting a real bad feeling about it. I mean, when you hear the house creak and groan, when the windows are rattling in their frames...fellers, it makes you feel pretty small and fragile.

Then the electric lights started blinking, and

Slim had a pretty good idea what was coming next. He hurried into the kitchen and rummaged through the cabinets until he found his kerosene lamp. He hadn't used it since the last time the power had gone out, so the lamp's glass chimney was covered with black soot, dust and mud dobber nests. He cleaned it and had just lit the wick when the power went out.

He shook his head and growled, "I'm never ready for these things, always half a step behind." His eyes grew wide. "Good honk, I'd better fill the bathtub in case my water freezes up!"

He dashed into the bathroom. Under normal conditions, we dogs follow our people from room to room, but on this deal, I wasn't sure that would be a good idea. I mean, we'd had an unfortunate incident in that same bathroom the night before and I had no wish to reopen old wounds.

But I did follow him to the door and watched as he turned the bathtub's water spigot. Two drips of water came out, then nothing. His head slumped. "No electricity, no water pump, half a step behind. Well, it looks like we're going to have a dry camp for a while."

Holding the lamp in front of him, he went back into the kitchen and rummaged through cabinet drawers until he found a flashlight. He found five of them, actually, but only one that worked.

That sent him into another grumbling tirade. "These stinking flashlights sit there in the drawer for two years, just waiting for the power to go off, and then they all drop dead at the same time. The only time a flashlight works is when you don't need it."

To teach the flashlights a lesson, he slammed the drawer shut as hard as he could. BAM! Too bad he didn't get his thumb out of the gap. He let out a yelp of pain, shook his hand for a solid minute, and even put the thumb in his mouth and sucked on it.

I turned my head so as not to add to his embarrassment. I mean, we dogs could tell many stories about our people, but this was one that didn't need repeating, a grown man sucking on his thumb. The poor guy was having a real bad evening.

CHAPTER TEN

A Sound in the Dark

Armed with the one flashlight on the ranch that worked, Slim went out on the porch to check the thermometer. It didn't take him long. He came flying back inside, hugging his arms and gasping for breath.

"Holy cow, you can't believe how cold it is! The temperature's down to ten degrees, and I'll bet the wind chill is twenty below zero. Everything's going to freeze up tonight."

Well, it was going to be a long night: no lights, no water, wind screaming, house groaning and popping, windows rattling, and tree limbs banging on the side of the house.

Slim fixed himself a sad little supper out of a can: sardines embalmed in mustard. He laid one of the dead fish on a stale cracker. It was so bad, he gagged on it, which explains his sudden burst of generosity. "Here Hankie, you want a bite?"

Was he serious? I'd been sitting there, watching him gag on the stuff, observing his face as it became a pinched prune, and now he was going to share it with ME?

Ha. No thanks. I'd had a few dealings with his sardines. I lowered my head, tucked up my tail, and went slinking into the living room. Behind me, I heard him grumble, "Dumb dog."

Fine. As we dogs often say, "Some cowboys need more ignoring than others." I would take dumb over sick any day.

Speaking of sick, he still hadn't found the deposit I'd left under his bed, but on the other hand...sniff, sniff...you know, sardines smell pretty bad at first, but after you get used to the first blast of dead fish smell...I found myself drifting back to the kitchen.

I mean, you never know. Past experience isn't everything. Just because every sardine you've tried was toxic doesn't mean that you won't become best friends with the next one.

I met Slim in the kitchen door. "Too late, Mister Fuss Budget, I ate 'em all."

Anyway, as I was saying, we dogs have to be

very cautious about the stuff our people try to feed us, because they will give us any kind of garbage. One of the keys to success in the Dog Business is to choose your food with care, and be very suspicious of anything that smells like a dead fish.

Your sardines are a high risk food category, don't you know, and the best answer to a sardine is Iron Discipline. So, yes, once again, Iron Discipline had saved me from a bad food experience.

It's pretty impressive that a dog could exercise so much self-control, isn't it? You bet.

Even though the stove was running at full blast, the house was getting colder. The icy wind penetrated every seam and crack, and you could feel a draft moving across the floor. Slim settled into his easy chair, covered up with a wool blanket, and started reading a book by the light of the kerosene lamp. Drover and I moved as close to the stove as we could, without starting a hair fire on our backs.

The wind roared. The house creaked and groaned. Tree branches scratched on the side of the house like frozen claws.

And then we heard a banging noise outside. That was the first indication that...well, I guess you'll find out, if you decide to go on with the story. To be honest, I'm not sure you should. I'm not at liberty to reveal any details at this point, but I must warn you that we're about to leave the gentle and easy parts of the story and move into...well, troubled waters, so to speak.

It gets scary, that's all I can say. You'll have to be the judge on whether you go on or not.

I sat up and glanced around. Drover was asleep. Slim was reading. He hadn't heard the sound, so I barked. His eyes rose from the book and stabbed me like a two-pronged fork. He was about to tell me to knock off the noise (I know him *so well*), but then he heard it too. He cocked his head and listened.

Bam. Bam. Bam.

"What in the world is *that*?" He threw off his blanket and went to the north window, parted the faded, dusty curtains, and looked outside. "The saddle shed door blew open." He scowled and rubbed his chin with a finger. "I know I closed it. I think I closed it. Huh."

You know the one thing he didn't think about? You'll find out soon enough. I didn't think about it either.

Even though it wasn't a long walk to the saddle shed, he put on his warmest winter clothes: a heavy wool coat with a fleece collar, his wool Scotch cap with the ear flaps, insulated gloves, snow boots, and a silk wild rag tied around his neck. The man was dressing himself for the coldest weather we'd ever seen on the ranch.

Good. I was proud of him for going to all that trouble, and I really wished him the best, because I had no intention of going with him. I mean, somebody needed to stay and guard the stove, right? You bet, and besides, I wasn't the one who'd left the door unlatched. That was one careless mistake he couldn't pin on his dogs.

Bundled up like a robot, he lumbered to the door. His hand closed around the knob and he pulled the door open. Frigid air rushed in and I could hear the roar of the wind outside. I moved closer to the stove and wished he would hurry up and shut the door.

He turned and looked at...well, he seemed to be looking at me, and that didn't exactly cause bells of joy to start ringing in my heart. I flattened myself against the floor, hoping that... well, that maybe he wouldn't see me and might forget that I was there.

"Hank, come on. You too, Stub Tail. Y'all need to make a pit stop, and a little exposure to that wind might tell you what a couple of pampered mutts you are."

Pampered mutts! I couldn't believe he'd said that.

"Hurry up, let's get this over with. Out!"

Oh brother. For several seconds, I studied my options: hide under the coffee table; dash down the hall and hide in his bedroom? No, any of those diversions would have merely inflamed the situation and made it worse.

I rose to my feet and gave Drover the boot. "Get up, soldier, we're going on a forced march. Rattle your hocks."

You never heard such moaning, whining, whimpering, squeaking, wheezing, groaning, and griping. "It's freezing out there! This leg's killing me! My tail's so cold, it'll hardly wag! Help, murder, my leg!" And so forth.

It did no good. Slim was waiting at the door, his face as stern as granite. He wasn't going to give us a pass on this deal.

When I stepped out on the porch, the wind hit me like a wall of ice. I'd experienced my share of cold winds before. I mean, this was the Panhandle, not Port Isabel, and we were accustomed to harsh winters. But THIS! Fellers, it was more than cold, more than bitter cold. It took my breath away and left me stunned.

This was *killer cold.*

Slim stepped off the porch and went trudging off toward the saddle shed, following the beam of his flashlight. I could have stayed on the porch with Mister Squeak and Moan, but the thought of listening to his noise just...I don't know, it overwhelmed me, I guess. I didn't think I could stand it.

And besides, going with Slim was the right thing to do. Slackers can sit on the porch and whine, but your top-of-the-line cowdogs stay with their people, through thick and thicker.

I stepped off the porch and caught up with him. He was humped over and trying to protect his face from bullets of ice, and every breath made steam in the air. He gave me a weak smile and said, "Pooch, this is how people froze to death in the old days."

Right. And there I was, right beside him, even though he'd hogged all the sardines.

These people have no idea how hard we work to please them.

By the time we reached the saddle shed, I was already half-frozen. We needed to get the door secured and return to base, but while we were there, I figured it wouldn't hurt to do a quick check of the shed. I mean, sometimes coons will

sneak into a shed and get into mischief, right? You bet, and coon mischief can be very destructive. So while the door was in the open position (it had been banging open and shut, don't you see), I darted inside.

Familiar smells reached my Noseatory Sensors, mostly alfalfa hay and horse feed, but I noticed another smell that wasn't so familiar, a kind of musky, oily smell. I sent that information to Data Control and while I was waiting for the results to come back, I saw a hairy, roundish, shadowy form sitting behind a bale of hay. Oh, and I could hear it chewing on something.

When the report came back from DC, I put the clues together and knew we had a Bingo. We had caught a thieving raccoon in the barn!

CHAPTER ELEVEN

Sure 'Nuff, We Found a . . . HUH?

How did I know it was a coon? Easy. Let's do a quick review of the Clue List.

Musky smell: Raccoons have a lot of oil on their hair and skin.

Roundish form: In the wintertime, coons get lard-fat and grow a heavy coat of hair, and the combination makes them about twice as big as they look in the summer.

Eating something: The "something" was horse feed, also known as "sweet feed." It contains oats and molasses, and coons love it. Who or whom would you expect to find stealing horse feed on a cold winter night?

Do you get it now? Heh heh. I had just walked into a burglary-in-progress and things were fixing to get exciting. I mean, scuffling with a coon can be a lot of fun when we've got a cowboy around to break up the fight in case it gets out of hand. A shovel works wonders in those situations—applied to the coon, don't you see.

The only question was whether the perp was my old pal Eddy the Rac or one of his thuggish cousins. The profile suggested someone quite a big bigger than Eddy, maybe one of his cousins, Harley or Choo Choo. I'd sparred a few rounds with those bums and they were pretty tough, but now, with Slim backing me up...

Just to be on the safe side, I tossed a glance behind me. The door had blown shut and my partner seemed to be struggling to open it in the wind. I waited. At last, he pried it open and I saw the glow of his flashlight.

"What you got, Hankie, a mouse?"

The sound of his voice gave me a rush of courage. A mouse? Oh no, much better than a mouse. I whirled back to the thieving raccoon and announced our presence with a jarring bark. "Hank the Cowdog, Special Crimes Division. Hands up and reach for the sky!"

I love doing that. It makes me feel so...so...so something. Strong. Stern. Powerful. Important. A figure of great authority. The Dog in Charge.

At that very moment, the beam of the flashlight landed on the...my goodness, that was a big coon, and he'd sure piled on the lard over the winter months.

That was a *real* big coon.

That coon was HUGE.

Slowly, he turned his head around: short muzzle, little green eyes, enormous teeth, and slobber dripping from his lips. I felt the hair rising on my back, and ten thousand volts of electricity shot down my spine and went all the way out to the end of my tail.

And then he growled. Coons don't growl like that. My eyes bugged out and my ears flew up.

Behind me, I heard Slim's astonished voice. "Good honk, that's a BEAR!"

Right. And then he roared. He didn't growl or grumble or snarl. He ROARED.

What happened at that point became a blur. We're talking about a "stampede amongst the yearlings," as the cowboys often say. Chaos, pure nerve-burning, eye-popping, spine-chilling chaos.

I hit Full Afterburners and headed for the door. So did Slim, only the door slammed shut in the screaming wind, and for a moment of heartbeats, it appeared that we were about to be eaten alive.

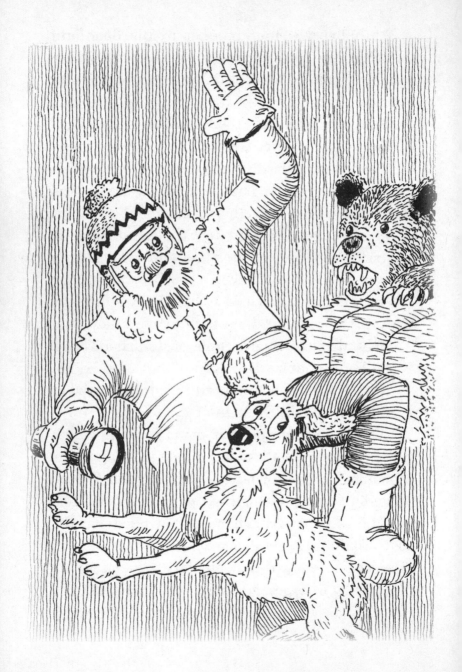

But Slim put his shoulder to the door and forced it open, and the two of us went flying outside, running for our very lives, and I can vouch that neither one of us gave the slightest thought to the bitter cold. Do you know why? *Because the bear was coming after us!* Over the scream of the wind, we could hear the thud of his feet on the frozen ground and the rumble of his growling voice.

I wish I could report that Slim and I made it to the house, barricaded the doors, and armed ourselves with knives and guns and swords, but you know, Life has its way of playing nasty tricks upon us.

I don't know how it happened...okay, maybe I know how it happened and it doesn't make me proud. See, in the sheer panic of the moment, I somehow got myself tangled up in his legs.

Hey, I didn't plan it that way. All I can say is that in moments of terror, a dog wishes to be as close to his human friends as possible, and...hang on, this is going to get REALLY SPOOKY. See, he didn't just fall on the ground. He lost his balance, started falling, and....

Gulp.

Okay, Slim had been running at full speed, but lost his balance and started stumbling toward the ground. If he'd only hit the ground, it wouldn't have been so bad, but he stayed on his feet just long enough to *run into a tree*. Head-first. Center-punched it and dropped like a sack of rocks.

This was bad. This was very, very bad.

The wind screamed, Slim was down, and I was...let's be honest here, suddenly I was overwhelmed by sheer terror and began doing the strangest things you can imagine: cackling with insane laughter, moaning, and barking in a random fashion. I dropped to the ground, flopped around, leaped up, and ran in circles.

And the bear kept coming...toward Slim.

It sounds hopeless, doesn't it? That's the way it looked to me, but then I experienced a moment of...how can I say this? I experienced a moment of calm and clarity. It seemed to come out of nowhere. All at once, I realized that this was... this was *a Halloween party and someone had dressed up in a bear suit*!

Yes, of course, why hadn't I thought of it sooner? Ha ha. Some guy had dressed up in a bear costume and he was trying to scare everyone, ha ha, and by George, he was doing a pretty good job of that, but it was all just a joke and if I ran to the porch and hid behind the wood pile, morning would come and it would all go away.

See, parties are just play-like stuff. They're not real. They come and go. It happens all the time, right? Sure it does, so, yes, I headed for the porch as fast as my legs would take me.

Slim would be fine, and tomorrow, we would share our memories and laugh around the wood burning stove. What a warm, wonderful scene it would be! A cowboy and his dog, laughing and sharing and building the bonds of trust.

I made it to the porch and was on my way to the woodpile, when I encountered...what was that? Oh, Drover, of course. He was sitting there like a statue, but with a look of horror on his face.

Over the howl of the wind, I yelled, "What's wrong with you? You look like you've seen a ghost."

"Not a ghost, a b-b-b-bear!"

"It's not a bear, Drover, it's some guy in a Halloween costume. Don't worry about it. Let's hide behind the wood pile, hurry!"

He didn't move. His eyes were glazed and they looked a little crazy. He gave his head a hard shake. "It's a bear...and Slim's in trouble." His eyes focused on me. "We've got to help him!"

"Drover, listen to me. This isn't real, it's...it's just a costume party, no kidding. All we have to do is hide and…"

The voice that came out of Drover's mouth sent chills down the back of my neck. It didn't sound like Drover's voice, or any voice I'd ever associated with him. It said, "If you won't help him, I WILL."

He leaped off the porch and vanished in the howling storm.

I was so shocked, I couldn't move or think. Had I been talking to Drover, and had he spoken the words I thought I'd heard? And had he actually raced out into the storm to…to do what he'd said he was going to do?

My mind swirled—thoughts, memories, faces, words, feelings—and above it all, I began hearing a frenzied, high-pitched yipping sound (Drover's barking), followed by a man's voice: "Hank, over here, I need you! Help!"

You know what? This is WAY TOO SCARY and I can't go on with it. You know me, I worry about the little children and…hey, let's be frank about this. It's too scary for me too! I mean, if the guy who's telling the story gets so spooked that he can't continue, what's left to do?

Let's just fold it up, brush our teeth, say our prayers, and go to bed, what do you say? Nightie night, and sweet dreams.

CHAPTER TWELVE

You're Supposed to be in Bed, Asleep

What's the deal? I thought we agreed to call it quits, but you're still reading. Maybe you were so worried about Slim and Drover that you couldn't sleep.

Me too. Who can sleep when his buddies are about to be eaten by a bear?

So here we are, wide awake and worried sick. Do we dare plunge on with the story? Here's an idea. Let's creep forward and see how it goes. If it gets too scary, we'll hide under the bed and...I don't know, eat crackers or something.

Let's give it a shot. Take a deep breath, we're moving out.

Okay, there I stood, alone on the porch, listening to the scream of the storm and the sound of my master's voice, calling for help.

And suddenly it all came back to me—who I was, where I was, and what had to be done. I stiffened my shoulders and tried to put some steel into my spine. That wasn't easy, because it had turned into wilted celery.

I turned into the wind, and gasped as it stole the breath right out of my body. In the distance, I could see the beam of the flashlight and a dimly-lit scene that might have come out of a nightmare: a man lying on his back with a pathetic, quivering little mutt beside him, and both of them watching the approach of a bear with two clawed hands raised in the air, and eyes that showed sheer menace.

This wasn't going to be fun.

I dived off the porch and went ripping into the night. Seconds later, I was standing beside Drover. "All right, men, lock and load! Drover, you take the right flank and I'll move in on the left side. We'll lay down some cover fire and try to hold his attention. Slim, you need to get off your duff and make a dash for the house. We'll be right behind you. Do you copy?" I turned to Drover. "Drover, check in. Do you copy?"

He looked at me with crossed eyes. "I'm so glad you're here! Now, I think I'll faint."

"You will NOT faint! Take the right flank and lay down some barks. Move!" I shoved him into position and somehow he managed to lay down some squeaks. The bear lunged at him and took a swipe at him with his paw.

That gave me just enough of an opening so that I rushed forward and clamped my teeth on a hind leg. I gave him a good bite, but it reminded me of biting a big fur coat: lots of hair and skin, not much meat.

But he felt it, and I paid a price. He gave me a backhand with his left paw, and fellers, I thought I'd been hit by a bus—ten feet through the air. But the good news about backhands is that you miss the claws. It knocked the wind out of me and, well, kind of hurt my pride, but I jumped up and got back into the fight.

I must say this about Drover. He was scared out of his mind and didn't do much but squeak and dodge, but he didn't faint or run for the house, and somehow the combination of my deep manly barking and his ridiculous squeaks kept the bear off balance and distracted.

Slim was able to drag himself off the ground, then he started chugging toward the house. When he made it to the porch, I heard his voice above the wind. "Okay, dogs, I made it! Head for the house!"

Well, he didn't need to repeat that command. I looked around for Drover and...why did I bother? I should have known. He was already high-balling it back to the house, moving like a little white comet. I followed, and seconds later, executed a smooth landing on the porch and saw Slim up ahead, holding the door open for me.

"Come on, pooch, inside! Nice work."

Yeah, well, we could talk about the "nice work" later. I shot through the opening and Slim slammed the door behind us. Whew! We had made it. We were alive and safe.

Slim wasted no time celebrating. He dashed to the telephone and dialed a number. "Sheriff's Department? This is Slim Chance. Tell Deputy Kile that his bear showed up at my house."

Suddenly we all heard heavy sounds on the porch. And the house began to tremble.

Slim swallowed hard. "Tell Deputy Kile that his bear's *on my front porch!*"

I happened to be looking at Drover when the bear started banging on the door. His eyes grew wide, crossed, and moved in circles. And then... this is going to scare the liver out of you, so hang on...then there was this loud crashing sound, and WE SAW A HANDFUL OF CLAWS coming through a hole in the door!

The bear had knocked a hole in the door and was reaching inside!

Slim did a double-take, then yelled into the phone, "Tell Deputy Kile the bear's coming into my house, and he needs to get down here double-quick!"

He slammed down the phone and stood there for a moment, blinking his eyes. Drover and I sat there like...I don't know what, but we were beyond scared, and all the while, we could hear the bear ripping a bigger hole in the front door.

Slim seemed to be in a trance, so...well, I had to take charge. When in doubt, a dog should always bark, and that's what I did—a loud, emphatic bark that had some iron in it. "Slim, snap out of it! A bear's coming through the door and you need to do something!"

His eyes came back into focus and he said, "Back door. Let's get out of here!"

Well, glory be! Great idea. 2.5 seconds later, Drover and I were lined up at the back door. Slim jerked it open and we went flying outside, just as the bear opened the front door and came inside.

So what do you do in this kind of situation? I mean, the horrible beast had chased us into the house, and now he'd chased us out the back door.

And don't forget that the chill factor that night was about twenty degrees below zero. To escape a killer bear, we had gone out into the killer cold.

Where do you go? Where do you hide? Slim and I had been through some bad scrapes together, but this one had all the markings of The End.

Do we dare plunge on with this story and go soaring into the Great Unknown? We've made it this far. Let's keep going.

Somehow in all the fear and tension of the moment, Slim came up with a sensible plan, maybe the only one available. I mean, running off into the night wasn't an option. We would have frozen to death in that cold, and then we would have become burgers for the bear.

Here's what we did. We crept around the south side of the house. Slim peeked around the corner. The bear had gone inside, so we made a dash for the pickup. Slim jerked open the…OH NO! The pickup door had frozen shut! How did that happen?

Easy. When you combine freezing drizzle with below-zero chill factors, machinery stops functioning. Motors don't start, windshield wipers don't wipe, and doors don't open.

We were locked out of our pickup, standing

out in the freezing cold! The bear heard our noise and came outside. He pinned his ears down and screamed a growl, went down on all-fours...and HERE HE CAME!

It sure looked like the end, but lucky for us, Slim had been through this frozen door business before and knew how to respond. He grabbed a shovel out of the back of the pickup, stuck the shovel blade into the crack between the door and the door frame, and pried upward. And holy smokes, it worked! It broke the seal of ice and he opened the door.

"Get in, dogs!"

We went flying inside the pickup, and so did Slim. His breath made clouds of fog and his hands were shaking. We all looked through the window and saw the bear lumbering toward us, roaring in anger and throwing punches in their air with his huge paws.

Slim said, "Let's get out of here!"

Great idea.

His gloved hand went to the ignition key. He turned the key. The motor turned over, groaned, gurgled...and quit! In the deadly silence, Slim said, "I should have parked it out of the wind. Nothing works in this cold."

We watched in petrified silence as the bear

loomed up beside Slim's door and brought his huge ugly face right next to the window glass. Nobody in that pickup wanted a close-up view of this monster, but we got it anyway, every detail of his nose, teeth, and vengeful little pig eyes.

He roared, he screeched, he banged on the window, and the only thing between us and a dreadful fate was that quarter-inch of window glass. It sounds hopeless, doesn't it? I mean, be honest, what were the chances that we'd get out of that deal alive?

Well, don't give up yet. We had exhausted all our ideas and were trapped in the pickup like rabbits in a pipe, but here's what saved our skins. In the process of roaring about all the things he was going to do to us if he ever got inside the pickup, the bear breathed hot breath on the window...and it *fogged up the glass*. The fog froze on the glass and he couldn't see us inside the pickup.

Incredible.

We could hear him out there, but couldn't see him, and even better, he couldn't see us. For a while, he growled and grumbled and banged on the fender, then...silence.

Slim found a little hole in the frost and peeked outside. "He's back on the porch. He's going inside the house. You know what? I'll bet he smells my sardines." Slim cocked his head and glanced around. "And you know what else? Bobby Kile just rolled up, and we might live to see another day."

Sure enough, a set of headlights cut through the darkness...no, two sets of headlights...three... holy smokes, Deputy Kile had brought a whole posse of deputies and officers, and fellers, they had arrived just in the nickering of time! It was our good fortune that they'd been out on patrol, looking for the bear, when they got a distress call from the sheriff's office on the radio.

Slim rolled down his window and there was Deputy Kile's grinning face. "We've had a complaint about a loud party in this neighborhood."

Slim laughed and shook his head. "Bobby, sometimes you're a pain in the neck, but this time...boy, am I glad to see you! The bear's inside my house."

We got out of the pickup and the men went right to work. Deputy Kile had done some research on bears, and he'd come with exactly the right weapon: an air rifle that fired a tranquilizer dart.

He crept up on the porch and peered inside. There, he saw the bear sitting on the floor, licking the juice out of the bottom of Slim's sardine can. Deputy Kile stepped into the doorway, raised the tranquilizer gun to his shoulder, and fired. It made a little popping sound. The bear felt a sting but kept on licking sardine juice. About two minutes later, his eyes began to sag. He yawned, curled up, and went to sleep.

Whew!

Getting the bear out of the house proved to be a lot harder than putting him to sleep, but the crew of deputies got it done. Four strong men dragged him outside and loaded him into a covered trailer that was stout enough to hold him.

Around eleven o'clock, Mister Half Grown Black Bear was on his way to the zoo in Oklahoma City, and we were huddled up in Slim's living room, listening to the wind and soaking up every bit of warmth from the wood stove.

Oh, by the way, Slim got the door patched up with duct tape, a cowboy's second-best friend, after baling wire.

Wow, what a finish, right? Who would have thought that we could survive such an ordeal? Are you feeling better now? I sure am, and I'm glad we were brave enough to mush on with the story.

Nice work. Brush your teeth, hit the sack, and have a nice dream. This case is closed.

Have you read all of Hank's adventures?

Join Hank the Cowdog's Security Force

Are you a big Hank the Cowdog fan? Then you'll want to join Hank's Security Force! Here is some of the neat stuff you will receive:

Welcome Package
- A Hank paperback
- An Original (19"x25") Hank Poster
- A Hank bookmark

Eight digital issues of
***The Hank Times* with**

- Lots of great games and puzzles
- Stories about Hank and his friends
- Special previews of future books
- Fun contests

More Security Force Benefits
- Special discounts on Hank books, audios, and more
- Special Members-Only section on website

Total value of the Welcome Package and *The Hank Times* is $23.99. However, your two-year membership is **only $7.99** plus $5.00 for shipping and handling.

☐ Yes I want to join Hank's Security Force. Enclosed is $12.99 ($7.99 + $5.00 for shipping and handling) for my **two-year membership**. [Make check payable to Maverick Books.]

Which book would you like to receive in your Welcome Package? (#) any book except #50

BOY or GIRL

YOUR NAME (CIRCLE ONE)

MAILING ADDRESS

CITY STATE ZIP

TELEPHONE BIRTH DATE

E-MAIL (required for digital Hank Times)

Send check or money order for $12.99 to:

Hank's Security Force
Maverick Books
PO Box 549
Perryton, Texas 79070

DO NOT SEND CASH. NO CREDIT CARDS ACCEPTED.
Allow 2–3 weeks for delivery.
Offer is subject to change.

The following activities are samples from *The Hank Times*, the official newspaper of Hank's Security Force. Please do not write on these pages unless this is your book. Even then, why not just find a scrap of paper?

For more games and activities like these, be sure to check out Hank's official website at **www.hankthecowdog.com**!

"Photogenic" Memory Quiz

We all know that Hank has a "photogenic" memory—being aware of your surroundings is an important quality for a Head of Ranch Security. Now you can test your powers of observation.

How good is your memory? Look at the illustration on page 48 and try to remember as many things about it as possible. Then turn back to this page and see how many questions you can answer.

1. Was Hank looking to HIS Left or Right?

2. Was Slim Asleep or Awake?

3. The window shade was down Half, Most of, or All the way?

4. What shape was the picture frame? Oval, Circle, or Rectangle?

5. How many of the DOGS' front legs could you see? 2, 3, 4, or all 5?

"Word Maker"

Try making words from the names below. Make up to twenty words with as many letters as possible.

Then, count the total number of letters used in all of the words you made. See how well you did using the security rankings below.

PROWLING BEAR

_____   _____

_____   _____

_____   _____

_____   _____

_____   _____

_____   _____

_____   _____

_____   _____

_____   _____

_____   _____

55-61   You spend too much time with J.T. Cluck and the chickens.

62-67   You are showing some real Security Force potential.

68-72   You have earned a spot on our ranch security team.

73+   Wow! You rank up there as a top-of-the-line cowdog.

John R. Erickson, a former cowboy, has written numerous books for both children and adults and is best known for his acclaimed *Hank the Cowdog* series. He lives and works on his ranch in Perryton, Texas, with his family.

Gerald L. Holmes has illustrated numerous cartoons and textbooks in addition to the *Hank the Cowdog* series. He lives in Perryton, Texas.